SEEDS OF DECEPTION

by

LeNora Millen

authorHOUSE

1663 Liberty Drive, Suite 200
Bloomington, Indiana 47403
(800) 839-8640
www.authorhouse.com

This book is a work of fiction. Places, events, and situations in this story are purely fictional and any resemblance to actual persons, living or dead, is coincidental.

© 2005 LeNora Millen
All Rights Reserved.

No part of this book may be reproduced, stored in a retrieval system, or transmitted by any means without the written permission of the author.

First published by AuthorHouse 02/19/05

ISBN: 1-4184-1635-5 (e)
ISBN: 1-4184-1634-7 (sc)
ISBN: 1-4184-1633-9 (dj)

Library of Congress Control Number: 2004093547

Printed in the United States of America
Bloomington, Indiana

This book is printed on acid-free paper.

DEDICATION

This book is dedicated to my brother "Pookie", I love you and miss your beautiful smile and adventurous stories

To the loving memory of my great grandmother "Mama Julia", my guardian angel

In memory of my beloved Aunt Kate

In memory of Papa Joe

In memory of Jake and LeNora Plummer

ACKNOWLEDGEMENTS

Thank you God for guiding me daily while on this journey and for giving me the strength, and the insight to forge ahead while at times facing doubt. The Goddess within was able to remove the barriers and allowed me to travel within the scope of the imaginable and unimaginable.

My precious parents, Robert and LaVerne Miller, I love you dearly. Thank you for instilling hope and courage to walk out on faith. Your encouraging words and prayers truly paved the way for my success.

My wonderful grandparents, Houston and Ruby Traylor, I love you so much. There are no words to describe my gratitude for the help and support you have given me throughout the years. I will always cherish the childhood fun and memories shared.

My son's Blake and Brian, my little soldiers. I love you unconditionally, remember to always keep your minds open in order for wisdom to knock at your door. Knowledge wasted is most definitely an insult to your intelligence.

My sisters and brothers, Tony, Joyce, Robbijon, Ruby and Pam. Much love to my "peeps". I really appreciate your words of wisdom and your help when I needed advice. Thank you all for giving me positive food for thought.

To Donald, I want to thank you for being such a wonderful friend and for being in my corner, most importantly, thank you for lending me a strong shoulder to cry on when I needed it. God Bless you, and may you have much success.

To Dr. Clifford Black and those Jonathan's who are soaring above this earthly plane and jetting toward mindless possibilities. Keep flying high and remember, "Chickens don't fly, they fry"!

To Arlene (Lucy) Davis, Matthew Patton, and the wonderful staff at AuthorHouse. The completion of this book could not have been possible without your help and guidance. I am so very fortunate to have worked with such a wonderful and dedicated group of individuals.

Thurman Northcross, divine intervention purposed itself towards our paths crossing. The Goddess within me truly sees the God within you. The Journey has now begun, welcome it!

SEEDS OF DECEPTION

Introduction

My name is Jessie Fremont... as I stared into the mirror this morning I gazed upon a reflection that can be found within the face of many—that reflection being sadness. There is a void in my life, an unending emptiness inside, which continually eats away at the core of my soul. Within the eyes of my mother I see my reflection, even in her smile. Yet there is a part of me I've not yet met or come to know. I've never really felt like a whole person and never will, until I find my father. This is what causes my sadness. Jessie Fremont is only a name, but my true reflection is the insurmountable foundation of my existence. This image of myself not only can be found within the mirrors of my life, but within the reflective mirrors of the man and woman who were responsible for my entire being. This life I did not ask for or create, yet I exist; a life uncertain, yet I exist; a life without a father, yet I exist; but for how long? How long will I have to stare into the sad eyes of my brothers and sister, and how long will I have to helplessly watch my mother destroy her life? My mother, a woman I love with all my heart whose absence has become an uninvited guest within our household. Its presence captures our childhood and suspends it within its ball of confusion and hopelessness. Our cries go unheard as we awake to hold only one another and breathe in the dusty air of loneliness instead of the essence of our mother's perfume. We struggle with our mother's absence and find comfort in knowing that she may return; at least we hope she does. Time passes slowly around here, especially when every minute is spent with worry, some days not knowing whether our mother will even walk back through the door... and as the clock slowly ticks, the days pass without hearing from her. Fear whispers in our ears as our hearts silently cry for her return, and again our cries go unanswered.

CHAPTER 1

Today is Wednesday. As the darkness of night approaches there is no sign of her. When she left a few days ago, she said she was going to the store to get some food. I knew in my heart that it would be several days before we would see her. She would often get drunk with her boyfriend Randle and not show up until she was sober, or when that no-good bum would kick her out. I did the best I could to keep our family together; Mom knew this and would often say, "Jessie since you are the oldest, you are in charge of looking after your sister and brothers when I'm not here. Do you understand?" But how could I, a fourteen-year-old, understand having their mother away from home more often than she was there? And how could I ever understand the hunger pains we continually felt? Worst of all, seeing the sad expression on my sister and brother's face, because our mother would disappear with no explanation at all. As a result of Mom's absence we have shed many tears, and comforted each other throughout the lonely nights.

At times I would want to crawl under a rock and lose my own existence because I felt that this would be my only escape. I found it difficult to survive at times because I've struggled within the realms of my own being and have tried to figure out why my mother's behavior has changed so drastically toward us, when all we are trying to give and show her is love.

Most of the children in the neighborhood, from what I see, seem to have their parents at home with them and want what's best for them. I know this to be true, because I would often hear them speak of the good times they would share with their parents. Some of them, such as myself, having only a single mother within the home, yet they seemed to have their mother as their mentor and guide. They would often boast about their mother's ability to keep food on the table and clothes on their backs. I somehow seemed to always be the outsider; oftentimes I would go into my little imaginary world and paint this picture of my mother to my friends as a super-mom. It hurt worse, because I knew that this was only a lie and that I would soon face the truth once I got home from school. At least my momentary world of picture-perfect home life put a smile on my face. Although I knew it was wrong to lie, I felt that somehow if I kept my faith and held on to this vision of my mother, that somehow, someway, I may greet this woman I imagine her to be. Someone once told me that without a vision, we perish. I refuse to give up on my family; therefore, I choose to cling to the hope that one day this lie would become a reality.

Why did this have to happen to us? Why my family? This question I've asked myself over and over again. Deep inside I know that she has feelings for us; I've seen and felt Mom's love—that is, before she met Randle.

One thing I found so difficult to understand was why Mom would not let us even attend church—at least we would have found some kind of comfort. Oddly enough, we didn't even have a Bible in our home. I soon let my mind drift back to the fateful Sunday morning that would set my destiny in motion. My best friend Patrick had invited me to attend church with him, and of course I was excited because I'd never set foot in a church. I'd always wondered about what went on in church; now I was finally going to get a chance to learn something about this almighty God I'd hear people praising and glorifying.

I was so excited that I don't think I got any sleep the night before. I got my clothes out early Saturday evening, I think I may have used a half a can of spray starch on my shirt and pants. I wanted to look my best in God's house. I really didn't have any nice church clothes, but I knew it didn't really matter. I thought about what Patrick once told me. He said, "You know, Jessie, God loves all of His children, and he knows who His children are. God is concerned with our hearts, and how we treat our fellowman. God is love, and He wants us to spread love in this world; He doesn't want us to hate one another or destroy what He has created." Patrick would stand like a soldier in battle holding his Bible under his arm; this he said was the only weapon he needed. He would make his voice sound deep like the preachers I'd see on television; he'd then wait on me to say, "Amen, brother, preach the word," and that would get him to preaching even louder.

Patrick was known for preaching and because of this he would always get picked on at school or even worse, chased home. Patrick's sense of humor would become his protector; he had this uncanny ability to charm people with his wit. He was a master at laughing at himself or turning the table on whoever chose to challenge him; sometimes pulling the bullies into his corner by his unusual way of what he called Patrick's psychology. "Don't bluff the bully," Patrick would say, "instead crush them with the mighty blow of the unexpected. The charm of it," he would say, "is to totally confuse them to the point of forgetting what the heck they wanted to beat the crap out of you for in the first place." It didn't matter to him whether he was called a coward as long as he could walk away in one piece. Patrick would sometimes say, "Boy, it's hard trying to be a Christian, maybe I should take up karate instead."

I understood Patrick; he was one of the first people to introduce himself to me when I moved into the neighborhood, and he's been my best friend since. I sort of looked up to him. Even though Patrick loved to preach, it never bothered me. I believe it may have been because he was teaching me something that I was never taught at home. One afternoon Patrick started preaching one of what he referred to as his eye opening sermons. He looked so serious as he stood on the top of his mother's porch; he had his microphone in his hand and his Bible under his arm. I found it impossible not to laugh at him: neighbors passing in cars found it impossible not to slow their vehicles once Patrick began his sermon. His voice could be heard on the entire block.

I found myself struggling to keep from laughing in his face. I looked away, all the while gritting my teeth in torture, while coughing in between laughter. I guess he must have thought I wasn't paying any attention; the next thing I knew he was asking me what he had preached about. I couldn't help but to laugh and say, "You expect me to repeat what you just said? You must be joking."

He looked at me all the while pointing at me with his Bible and said, "Jessie, I don't joke when it comes to my preaching." I could tell by Patrick's expression that he expected me to be a student of his word, as he would so often say. Before I could answer he said, "Jessie, don't think for one minute that I'm letting you off the hook."

At that moment I couldn't contain my laughter, especially when I thought about Patrick's facial expressions as he preached. He'd spread his nostrils as if to breathe in all the air his skinny little body could muster and he'd twist his mouth as if he were chewing on horsemeat. Then he'd begin his sermon, I don't know whose voice he was mimicking but he sounded as if he were talking with a sock in his throat.

I must have rubbed Patrick the wrong way because when I tried to tell him the reason I couldn't stop laughing, he totally ignored me; his only words to me were, "Tell me, Mr. Fremont, what did I preach about? I know you had to be paying attention since you claim you want to know more about religion."

I knew that I had to save face. Amazingly enough, this unknown God Patrick preached about must have found favor in me on that day, because I was able to actually repeat to my self-proclaimed preaching buddy most of his sermon. I was even able to use some of his charm on him. I told him that one day I may be sitting out in his church listening to him preach one of those fiery sermons that would make some of those women with the big hats want to shout and dance down the aisle.

Patrick laughed and said, "They can shout all they want to, as long as they don't fall on me and squash me like a pancake." Patrick's eyes lit up as he spoke. I knew instantly that he was going to tell a joke. He said, "Jessie, I remember being told about a lady who jumped up in church one Sunday and suddenly screamed out, 'Oh my God, Lord, help me.' She blacked out right after that. The people in the church said they thought she was filled with the holy ghost; come to find out she had a girdle on that was too tight; the pain finally got to her, and that's why she jumped up, hollered and fainted. They tell me she jumped five feet off the floor. Her girdle was later found behind the pulpit.

Patrick and I really got a good laugh off of that one. Patrick at the age of 15 stood six feet tall; he had several girls with crushes on him, but for some reason he ignored them. Because of Patrick's height, the basketball coach felt Patrick would have been a good player; of course, Patrick chose the chess team. He was fascinated with mental challenges and often spoke about his future as a scientist discovering cures for diseases such as diabetes, cancer, and sickle-cell. He once told me that he had lost an aunt to sickle-cell and it was difficult for him at the age of six to understand her dying. Tears welled up in his eyes as he talked about her; he said his mother would lose sleep some nights tending to his ailing aunt. Looking down at the ground as he shuffled the dirt and rocks under his foot, Patrick smiled and said, "Man, I guess that's why I try to preach; Mom and Dad went to so many revivals with my aunt that I started to mimic the preachers. I like the attention I get, especially from the girls."

I laughed, and said, "Man, you're gonna get kicked out of the church, anyway, what are you gonna call your church, Playa Playa Baptist Church, Rev. Slick residing?"

Patrick looked up side my head and said, "Man, I would pack a church, I don't have to be slick, I'll just be myself, just spellbinding."

Biting into my candy bar, I said, "Rev. Slick, I can see it now, you standing behind the pulpit telling one of your jokes while you're supposed to be preaching."

Patrick started laughing and said, "like my dad says, Jessie, if it's God's will I'll be a preacher, for all we know it may be you."

I asked Patrick to tell me more about baptism since he said he was already baptized. He scratched his head and said, "Jessie, you already believe; that's a start and through baptism our soul is cleansed.

I was confused and asked him whether it was like taking a bath." Before Patrick could answer, I said, "In that case, I can baptize myself."

Patrick smiled and said, "No way, Jessie, now I would hate to find my buddy drowned in the bathtub trying to baptize himself, man with that nose on your face it would take a week to pull it out of the drain." Patrick couldn't let that sense of humor go wasted; he was a regular comedian. He always found a way to make me forget what I was afraid of by turning the situation into something funny. Patrick told me that baptism was sacred and that we would talk more about it when we had time to meet with his minister. He felt that his minister could explain baptism to me in order for me to get a better understanding of it. He said that one of his greatest teachers was his dad, and that he and his dad had Bible study on the nights his father didn't work late. Patrick and his dad Pop were going fishing in a few days and I was invited to come along. I hesitantly told Patrick that if my mom didn't need me at home I'd be there. I knew that my chances of going with them would be slim. Either mom would say I couldn't go because I had to stay home and look after my two brothers and sister or she'd not be there and I'd be forced to. Patrick was really lucky to have both of his parents at home with him. He once told me that he and his family prayed for my family and that he knew that God would soon be answering those prayers. At that moment I thought to myself, what is Mom going to say when she finds out about what I'm planning to do? She should be happy that I'm learning something new, especially religion, but deep within I knew what her reaction would be. God knows I loved my family and would cringe at the thought of anything happening to them, I was their protector and I thanked God everyday for them. Although we had so many problems at home, I somehow knew that through the prayers of Patrick's family, God would make it better one day; it had to get better. My faith was the substance of my own survival.

Sunday morning greeted me with the unexpected. Mom told me that I wasn't stepping foot in church because I had to watch the children. I tried not to get angry, but ended up raising my voice at Mom. I asked her why I could never do anything with my friends or go anywhere.

She didn't say anything, so I kept talking. Although fear was kicking me in the butt, I told her that I was her son, not her husband or babysitter. What did I say that for, Mom's eyes looked as if they turned fire red, I knew my mouth had landed me in hot water. She slapped me so hard across the face that I felt the snot fly out of one of my nostrils. Mom was so angry that her voice trembled as she spoke. She told me that if I ever raised my voice at her again or showed any disrespect toward her, I wouldn't live to see 15 candles on a cupcake.

By that time there was a knock at the door; it was Patrick. I headed toward the door to tell him why I couldn't go to church, before I could get there Mom was telling him that he could go on to church without me, because I had more important things to do. Patrick's eyes met mine before I could hide my tears. He sort of sighed and said, "I'll see you later, Jessie." Trying to hide my embarrassment, I only nodded my head.

Mom slammed the door behind him as hard as she could. I knew at that moment that I was not going to give up on God. The battle had just begun. I also knew that my best friend Patrick was not going to give up on me. Somehow, someway I felt that through Patrick, God was directing me and helping me to be stronger for my sister and brothers. More importantly, my mother, who was slowly drifting away from us. I daydreamed about the laughter that used to fill the walls of the dingy house we lived in; somehow I had to find a way to recapture the happiness within the heart of my family; tears had become all too familiar within our household. I'm too young to be carrying the load of a son and fill-in father; I don't know how much more of this I can take, or any of us for that matter. Yesterday I existed, but today I choose to live for my family and I pray that my mother can become the person I want her to be, a loving mother to us again and I also pray that she finds herself through the reflectors she's created, her children.

The pain of how Mom treated us was evident, but we loved her in spite of odd behavior. I would sit up all night waiting on her to come home. Sometimes I would find her on the doorstep, drunk and beaten. Her boyfriend Randle would usually get drunk with her. I thought he was on drugs, because I had seen him come out of a crack house. I told mom, but she only got angry; and told me to mind my own business. I tried to explain to her that I was afraid that he might kill her because he beat her so bad once that we thought she was going to have to be put in the hospital.

Randle had a terrible temper; he once threatened to kill mom, and us, too! We had to run to the neighbor's house and call the police. Mom violently slapped me around, because she said I had caused her boyfriend to get arrested. I tried to tell her that I was only trying to help; she said she wanted me to leave her and her man alone. Mom said she was going to get on with her life, but because of us, no man wanted to marry her. She said we were not going to get in her and Randle's way like we had done with the other men. It was evident that Randle was the problem. Mom started drinking and staying away from home after she met him. Her whole attitude seemed to change; she acted as if she didn't care about anything, not even herself. She eventually stopped taking care of herself, becoming more and more self-destructive. I don't know why she loved him so much, anyway; I've seen people treat animals better than he treated Mom. Mom would sometimes try to fight back; I remember she once tried to fight back, because he beat her for not cooking. Mom threw a glass at him. Randle tried to catch it and it shattered in his hand, cutting some of his fingers. He got so angry that he started choking Mom. Carmen was screaming to the top of her voice; Willie and Aaron were pulling his legs, he swung at me twice but I knew with him being drunk his balance was off. I kept ducking and pleading with him to please leave my mother alone. I tried to explain to him that she was just trying to protect herself. He finally let go of her neck, she was coughing and gagging and her eyes were puffy and red. I wanted to kill Randle that very moment, I really did. Randle knew I didn't like him, yet he had enough nerves to ask me where the Band-Aids were. Out of breath and trying to gather my thoughts, I arrogantly said, "I don't know. Right now I'm trying to see whether Mom is all right. I sent Willie in the kitchen to get her some water. Randle yelled out again, "I said I need something for my fingers. Can't you see that your crazy mammy has made me cut my damn fingers?"

Aaron was afraid of him and said, "I know where they are," and he quickly ran in the bathroom. Randle slumped in behind him. I prayed for God to give me strength to respect this shell of a man, who for some strange reason had my mother blinded by what I guess she thought was love. If this is what love is I don't want or need it. After all of the drama and commotion, I was finally able to get Carmen quiet.

I knew that we could not keep watching our mother waste her life away as she was doing, but how could I ever get her to stop drinking and away from Randle? I knew she desperately needed help, but I didn't know the direction to take to get her to the help. If Mom only knew how much we needed her. What in God's name had caused her to become so bitter toward us? I sometimes wished I had never been born. Because of these feelings, I got fed up with everything and ran away from home. The only reason I went back was because I came to my senses and wondered what would happen to Carmen, Willie and Aaron; they were too young to be struggling without their mother, even worse their big brother. Carmen was only five, Willie was seven and Aaron was ten. If I were not there to take care of them they probably would not survive, or be taken away from Mom and sent to some strange foster home. I knew I couldn't turn my back on them. To make matters worse, Mom would be so drunk half of the time she didn't even know who she was; she sometimes would stay gone for weeks. We'd often have to skip school—that is, until the principal started asking questions about our absences, questions that we couldn't answer.

It was so stressful at home, I couldn't even concentrate on my homework. It was even more difficult for Willie and Aaron. They would try to give it their best shot, even though their little minds were filled with fear and worry.

At times, we'd be too weak and hungry to study. I remember we got so hungry once that I stole food from Mr. Charlie's store. Mr. Charlie caught me the second time and I begged him not to call the police. Patrick's dad happened to walk in the store that evening; he and Mr. Charlie were good friends. From the angry expression on Mr. Charlie's face, Patrick's dad knew something was wrong. He looked at me immediately and asked how I was doing, I hunched my shoulders and hesitantly told him what had happened. I felt so ashamed; it was even more difficult to even look them in the face. I promised them that it wouldn't happen again. I apologized repeatedly to Mr. Charlie for stealing out of his store. Mr. Charlie told me that if I ever got that hungry, just ask him, don't take from him. He said he'd go broke like that. Patrick's dad Pops expressed his disappointment and promised me that he and would send us some food whenever we needed it. He told me not be too proud or ashamed to ever ask for help. He was right, but I know that one of the biggest reasons for not asking was trying to cover up for Mom, because of her not being home with us. I knew sooner or later someone would start to ask questions about Mom's whereabouts. I didn't want her to get in trouble, so I decided it was best to skip school in order to protect her. Not once, but twice someone from the school came to the house;

we didn't answer the door and sat as quietly as we could. We didn't move until we knew they had finally gone.

This time Mom stayed away so long that I was forced to go to the police station. My worst fear was that something tragic had happened to our mother. Instead I found her asleep on the front porch the next morning. I guess Randle, the deadbeat whiskey-head, must have left her there; or worse, she may have walked clean across town from where he lived. He often got angry with Mom and would make her walk home.

She looked terrible. Who was this strange woman I was staring at? Momma used to keep herself clean, and she always kept her hair and nails done. Even though she really couldn't afford to go to the beauty shop she somehow scraped up enough money to fix herself up. She made sure she looked her best. Momma was once a beautiful woman, but no more, since she started drinking. She soon lost interest in her appearance; she started to use cuss words at us every opportunity she got. She looked and acted like a completely different woman. Her attitude got so bad that we would be afraid to say anything to her unless she spoke first. Worst of all, Momma almost lost her job because she kept showing up late for work. She was later put on probation; it was later recommended that she take an extended leave of absence. I still can't help but to blame Randle for Mom's problems. I felt that she did not care anything about the life God had given her, or our lives, either. I knew that I was not supposed to hate anyone, but I hated Randle. I would even pray to like him, but I guess my heart wasn't right yet because I felt like punching him out every time I saw him.

The neighborhood we lived in was no better; I always told myself that I would someday make enough money to move my family away from all the violence that we had to put up with. It wasn't even safe to walk to school, because of worrying about being robbed or confronted by gangs. One reason I was so afraid of them was because I had heard about them gunning a boy down in front of his home because he would not join what they called their organization, word out on the streets was that he was joining their rival gang. Even if a person chose not to join either gang, their life would still be in danger. Just about every kid in the neighborhood was afraid of them, even some of the adults. It was common knowledge that this gang had robbed and murdered several people in our neighborhood. Eventually, some of the neighbors got fed up and reported them to the police department. Their lives were soon threatened; one of the neighbors was shot in both his legs. In the midst of fear for their lives, as well as their family members, most of the neighbors decided to drop charges. Some of them had complained repeatedly to the police about being harassed by these little thug gangbangers. They didn't really have any other choice due to gang retaliation. This caused a lot of other people in our neighborhood to keep silent. I hope and pray that I never run into them on the streets because I know I would be in for a life-or-death situation. Just last night we heard gunshots outside our bedroom window; we hid under the bed; my little sister Carmen started to scream and yell for Mom; my two brothers only shook with fear. I knew I had to protect them, but I was scared, too. The shooting finally stopped but my heart was still beating fast, as I looked at my sister and brothers I knew that they felt my love and concern for them and that I would always be there to protect them. Even though I was only fourteen they looked up to me as if I was their father instead of their big brother. After all, I was the only father they knew.

Things only got worse around the house, such as when Mom's paycheck's stopped coming and the lights were cut off, especially when we had no food. I would sometimes dance for the money. Momma said I was a good dancer and I had missed my calling, but I knew deep inside that my calling was something more important than dancing on the streets for a few dollars. Sometimes I would wash cars for a few extra dollars or mow lawns in the neighborhood. My main concern was trying to hold my family together. They needed me and I needed them—as far as I knew we had no other family. My mother said she was the only child and that her parents had disowned her for something she had done in her past—she never said what it was.

Sometimes we would ask about our grandparents, and Momma would angrily say never to ask her about her parents, and for all she knew they may be dead. I remember Aaron once asked what our grandparents' names were and my mother looked at my brother and told him he didn't need to know. Aaron asked why. Momma, gritting her teeth, said, "Because I said so, and don't any of you as long as you live under my roof ever mention the word 'grandparents' to me again. Do you understand? You have no one but me."

Soon after this episode my mother went into the kitchen and started crying. I went in to try to talk to her; it hurt to see her so angry and sad all the time. She screamed for me to get out and leave her alone. I took Carmen, Willie, and Aaron into the bedroom, and told them to sit still until I got back. I knew Carmen would get very upset and somewhat agitated whenever Momma got drunk and started to scream all over the house. I closed the bedroom door and told them to stay there and play with their toys. I knew that Momma was going to sit at the table and try to drink her problems away, so she thought, and I would have to try to get her on the couch—that's usually the farthest I could take her. Momma needed help and I continued to worry about her drinking and how abusive she was toward us whenever she got drunk. My biggest fear was how I saw my mother's life wasting away every time she took a swallow of what I called "poison" and what the liquor store called "whiskey."

As I headed toward the kitchen I heard a loud crash. I quickly ran in and found Mom blacked out on the kitchen floor. I sent Aaron next door to call an ambulance. I panicked and kept putting a cold towel on Mom's face—she never came to. Mom was rushed to the hospital. At first I didn't think she was going to make it. The doctors told her that she wasn't going to survive unless she put the bottle down completely. What scared me the most was when Mom was told that she had just about destroyed her liver and that she had to choose life and seek help in her alcoholism or keep drinking and die.

In the days to come, I saw Mom go through mood swings, even crying uncontrollably at times. Each time I'd leave the hospital I'd suffer along with mother. I don't think I had any tears left to shed. It frightened me to see her hooked up to all of the tubes—they were in her nose and arms. Mom had also lost a lot of weight and her hair had also started to fall out. I prayed daily to God to help my mother. I didn't want her to die; she had to live for us; what would we do without her? On my last visit Mom repeatedly complained about the IVs in her arms and not wanting to eat any more of the hospital food. The nurse explained to Mom that she was on a special diet and that she had to eat the foods sent to her room. Mom would often raise her voice at the nurses, once causing a doctor to be called because Mom refused to eat and would often throw her food on the floor. To make matters worse, I was told that Mom would often cuss at the staff and had become somewhat of a nuisance, not only to the staff, but the patients, as well. The doctor was no pushover and told Mom that he would not tolerate her behavior, and in the event she disrespected the staff and disturbed any more of the hospital's patients, he would not hesitate to release her from his care. Mom knew that Doctor Blake was once of the best; therefore, she soon got her act together and apologized not only to Doctor Blake but also to the nursing staff she had offended.

I had not visited Mom for about a week because I had to take mid-semester exams. I'd gone to the principal's office and was permitted to leave early that day in order to visit Mom at the hospital. Upon reaching the hospital I immediately rushed toward Mom's room. As I entered the door, I was pleased to see that her appearance was improving, she appeared to be resting peacefully. I didn't want to wake her and leaned over and laid the get-well cards on the table that Carmen, Aaron and Willie had made her. I lifted up the lid on her dinner tray and was happy to see that she had eaten just about everything on it. In my haste to be as quiet as possible, I ended up knocking her water pitcher on the floor.

The sound startled Mom, quickly waking her. She looked at me and only smiled—her eyes appeared weak. The first thing she asked me was how I was doing. I didn't want her to worry any more than she had to so I told her that I was doing fine, even though I was terribly worried about her. I knew she would be asking about Carmen and my brothers, so I told her that they were at Mama Rose's. I knew Mom would feel at ease knowing that Mama Rose was taking care of us while she was recuperating in the hospital.

I asked Momma whether she would be coming home soon, explaining to her about how much we missed her. Mom smiled and said, "Son, Momma will hopefully be home real soon. I'm just waiting on the doctors to give me the day that I can walk out of these hospital doors feeling like my old self again."

Mom was full of questions, wanting to know about her dear friend Mama Rose, and whether we were doing as we were told. I told Momma that Mama Rose had sent her blessings and wanted her to know that we could stay with her until she got better. Mom suddenly started crying. She kept saying over and over, "This is not how I want to end up, Jessie." She started apologizing for all the pain she had caused us.

I tried to be strong as I felt my emotions surface. It hurt to see my mother in so much pain. I ended up crying and told her that we all just want her to hurry up and get better because we wanted her back at home with us. Mom grabbed my hand and told me that she needed us to help her because she felt she couldn't do it alone. She told me that she was really afraid and that she was willing to fight to get out lives back on the right track.

Looking me directly in my eyes, Mom promised me that she would get professional help as soon as possible. The doctors at the hospital had already given her a list of counselors to contact and had given her some literature to read on alcoholism.

CHAPTER 2

In the weeks ahead, Mom was finally released from the hospital. She was told to get plenty of rest and to keep the counselor's number near the telephone when she felt the urge to drink.

I helped out around the house as much as I could, even missing days from school that I shouldn't have. Some days, too tired to get Willie and Aaron dressed because I'd be too exhausted. Watching Willie, Aaron, Carmen, and Mom around the clock had physically wiped me out. Like a boxer at times, I felt beaten physically and emotionally, but I knew that I had to do what I could to keep my family going.

Fearful of Mom slipping off to see Randle, I kept a watch on her as much as possible. I tried to stay focused but I had continued to worry about our situation at home. Mom had not contacted any of the counselors the doctors at the hospital had referred her to. This concerned me more than anything. I knew I had to take matters into my own hands; so therefore, I was going to suggest to her in a non-threatening way that she contact someone for her drinking as soon as possible.

I didn't realize how much time had passed in trying to get our situation in order at home. This time we were out of school for almost two weeks, I knew that Momma would have to come to school to get us back in. I was glad that she was sober for a change. Carmen was running a fever, and Momma told us that Carmen might have the measles. I just hoped she stayed sober long enough to know that her children loved and needed her no matter how angry we made her.

When I got to school Monday morning, I was told to report to the principal's office. I was immediately directed to Mr. Moore's office; he was the school guidance counselor. As I entered his office, Mr. Moore looked at me and said, "Sit down, young man."

My mind was full of thoughts and questions, too! Were they going to kick me out of school? Did some of the neighbors call the school on us and tell them we were playing hooky? What?

Mr. Moore didn't waste any time explaining to me why I had been called in his office. He wanted to know why all of us had been missing school so often. I was also told that our absences were questionable. In a stern voice Mr. Moore looked at me and said, "Jessie, I'm concerned with you, son, because I've noticed that your grades are dropping. You have come from being an honor student to being almost at the average level in some of your subjects. He went on to say, "Son, I know that students sometimes cut class, even lie about their homework, but not you. You've always excelled in your studies. Now your mind seems to be clouded by something. I don't notice the spark in your eye, son. You were always such a friendly young man; now you don't even speak to me; you look straight through me and straight past me. I've also noticed as of late you walking around with a worried look on your face, with your head down most of the time. The only time I see any type of excitement in you is when your friend Patrick and his buddies come around. Otherwise, you walk around like a zombie."

Mr. Moore leaned back in his chair, his muscular body beginning to perspire as he shuffled through the papers on his desk. I sat quiet, wondering what his next line of questioning would be. I almost felt like I was being interrogated. Picking up his coffee cup, he seemed to be examining the contents before speaking, then said, "Jessie, I need to know what's going on in that head of yours. I know that you have a brilliant mind when you put it to positive use; it only needs to be tapped into." Mr. Moore took a deep sigh, not speaking, but just looking quite concerned. He leaned in my direction, looking directly in my eyes and said, "I'm not letting you waste your mind or your young life away with unnecessary stress, or an early ulcer, if I can help it. All I want to know is whether everything is all right at home with you and your mother? I hear that she has been in the hospital. Is this true, son?"

My mind was racing. Mr. Moore was really good at his job, or was I that transparent? I wanted to scream out to him. I wanted to cry on his shoulder, and say "Mr. Moore, you're right. Oh, you're so right." I thought to myself, "Finally I can tell someone about what was happening to us at home."

I must have been in a daze, because I heard Mr. Moore say, "Jessie, are you all right? You looked like you were going to black out on me."

"I'm all right, Mr. Moore," I quickly replied. "Everything is fine at home. We missed school because we were sick. It must have been a virus or something, because we all had the same symptoms."

Mr. Moore was no fool! I could tell he wasn't buying my story. He looked at me without batting an eye and said, "Jessie, I checked on Willie and Aaron's grades, too; the same thing is happening with them—their grades are dropping. I've been told that Willie has started to pick fights in class, and he seems to be a nervous wreck. Willie's teacher, Mrs. Hill, is very concerned about this unusual behavior she's witnessing. Mrs. Hill has informed me that Willie has always been one of her best students." Mr. Moore looked at me again and said, "Jessie, do you want to tell me something, son?"

I just hunched my shoulders and said, "I don't have anything to tell, sir."

Mr. Moore leaned over and picked up the folder on his desk and said, "By looking at this report I would say that Aaron's grades are also dropping. His teacher says he cries a lot on the playground and he isolates himself from his classmates now." Mr. Moore sat quiet for a few seconds, almost as if he was giving me the opportunity to confess. Still looking me directly in the eye, he said, "Son, I have been a counselor for twenty years and I taught school for eight; I know that what I'm seeing and hearing about you kids has nothing to do with a virus. Forgive me if I'm wrong, but I've been in this profession too long to let you walk out of my office with what you've been telling me this morning. I'm here to help you, son, not hurt you. I want to help you and your family; this includes your teachers, as well as the principal of this school. We are all here to extend help to your family when and if the need arises."

Mr. Moore continued to fight for my trust. He reached for his glasses, pulled out his handkerchief and neatly wiped them clean before placing them back on his face. Clearing his throat, he said, "Whether you want to believe it or not, it's true. Your education is very important. This is your future, son. Do you understand? Hear me and let it sink in."

As Mr. Moore spoke, I found it difficult to fight back my tears. It seemed that this miraculous God I heard people marvel about had begun to answer my prayers. We did need help; my entire family needed help. Mr. Moore looked at his watch, thirty minutes had passed, he took a deep breath and handed me an envelope and said, "Son, I want you to take this home to your mother. I will be waiting to hear from her no later than Wednesday. If she has not contacted me by then, I will come to your house to talk to her."

"God," I thought to myself, "I pray that Momma shows up, and I pray that she's sober." Somehow I felt like, maybe through Mr. Moore, Momma might be reached, but for how long?

Mr. Moore asked me whether I had any questions. "No, sir," I replied as I walked toward the door.

Mr. Moore reached out to shake my hand; I was hesitant because the palms of my hands were so sweaty, I guess from nervousness. "Have a good day, son, now don't let me down," he said as I wiped the sweat from my forehead.

"I won't let you down, Mr. Moore," I said as I left his office. It felt as if a weight had been lifted; forming an alliance with Mr. Moore was what I needed in order to help my family.

When we got home from school that afternoon, Momma and Carmen were asleep on the couch. I had already pulled the envelope out of my math book to give to her. I wondered what Mr. Moore had written on the paper. I knew it had something to do with our school grades and unexplained absences. I was pretty sure about that. I laid the envelope on the table next to the couch where Momma was sleeping. She looked so peaceful as she slept. I couldn't help but to stare at her. Mom was such a beautiful woman, and was beginning to look like the mother I thought I had lost at one point in our lives. I felt my feet slowly drift toward Mom and quietly bent down and kissed her on the cheek as she slept.

I gave my little sister Carmen, who was asleep next to Momma, a kiss, too. God forbid she somehow sensed that she was left out; not Carmen—she indeed took center stage. We would often say that Carmen demanded attention, and that one day she would grace the stage with her beautiful little voice. It was quite ironic that Mom had given her the name Carmen. I reached over and felt Carmen's forehead to she if she had cooled off since this morning; I was somewhat relieved to she that she was getting better. She had been burning up with fever when I left for school this morning.

Silence in the house was interrupted by voices coming from the bedroom—Willie and Aaron had started to joke each other about something; whatever it was, it made them laugh so hard that I had to tell them to be quiet before they woke Momma. It was indeed a pleasant change to hear a little laughter, any type of joy, in the house, because we had been at each other's throats so much lately. Most of the time it would happen whenever Randle would show up. He seemed to always welcome trouble, always bringing gloom and doom with him. He was like the Devil himself. I wondered what had happened between him and Momma, he had not been over, since they got into a fight at his apartment and he made Momma walk home. Maybe Momma finally came to her senses and realized that she was too good for him, and he was no good for her. For whatever reason he wasn't here, I didn't care. Momma did better when he was not around, anyway. We already knew that he didn't like any of us. We'd heard him say it several times; he always considered us to be excess baggage to him. Willie was so afraid of Randle that he cried if Randle even looked at him sideways.

Momma, on the other hand, treated us better when Randle was not around, and she didn't drink as much, either. She acted like she was afraid to show any affection toward us when he was around, maybe out of fear of him not loving her. Deep inside I knew Momma had to care—she really had me confused. Why did she allow this man to control her life like this? He was not worth it. He was pulling Momma down a tunnel of destruction, and if she didn't get a grip on her life soon, I didn't know what was going to happen to any of us! I was afraid. I'd never been so scared in my life.

My thoughts were suddenly interrupted by movement in the kitchen. As I walked in, I was greeted by Mom, who had awakened from her nap. She held a glass in her hand—my heart suddenly dropped. I focused on the liquid in the glass. God, I thought to myself, let it be water, anything but that poison Randle has been intoxicating her with. She was to blame, too, I thought. How could she have allowed herself to stoop to his level? As my eyes searched the glass, I blurted out, "What are you drinking, Mom?" Mom looked sort of puzzled, then said, "It's only water, son."

Feeling sort of awkward for questioning Mom, I remained silent as I breathed a sigh of relief. Mom finally broke the silence by asking me how my day had been at school, "All right, Momma," I said, "Mr. Moore, the guidance counselor at school, talked to me this morning. He sent an envelope home for me to give to you. He said if you have not contacted him by Wednesday, that he's coming to the house to talk to you."

Mom's face changed from calm to serious; she wanted to know why he needed to talk to her and what for? I told her about what Mr. Moore and I had discussed earlier that day. I also reminded her of the weeks we missed school when she was in the hospital and of the times we were out even before she was admitted to the hospital. My mission at that point of the conversation was to approach her in a way that she would understand the seriousness of her drinking problem. Although difficult, I had to reopen Pandora's box; our family had come too far to give up on Momma now. Weighing my words carefully, I reminded Mom of her irrational behavior reminding her in a gentle way that she had not been herself lately. I told her how much we had worried about her, especially since she had started drinking, and how we had not been getting our homework because we were too tired to go to school. I told her that with her being gone for weeks at a time, we had to skip school. "Someone had to watch Carmen, Momma," I said. "At times I would send Willie and Aaron to school, and I would stay home with Carmen since you were not here, but the principal had started asking questions that they couldn't answer. We had to protect you anyway we could. Momma, do you understand that we stayed out of school because we love you too much to see you arrested and locked up for child neglect or child abuse, whatever they call it? You were too drunk to know any of this. Many nights we couldn't sleep because we were too worried about you to think about sleeping."

Momma only stared; tears began to well up in her eyes. Silence again filled the room. Once I started to speak, I didn't think I would ever stop, there was so much that I needed to say, so many thoughts that I needed to express, things I felt Momma really needed to know and hear. I knew the most important thing was to get help for Mom's drinking problem. Gambling on her staying sober on her own was not reliable enough. The odds were already stacked against her, and with that no-good Randle as her drinking coach, this only put all of us in a no-win situation.

Before I had time to gather my thoughts, I blurted out, "Momma, you need to get help as soon as possible because you have become very abusive toward us." I kept talking because I wanted to make sure Momma understood our pain. "Momma, when we disobeyed you or talked backed, you usually would get the belt out and spank us if you felt like punishment was enough. Now, Momma, you're using your fist on us, you're slapping us around, even worse, Momma, you've started to cuss us out every time you get angry." Once my mouth got to moving I refused to stop talking, "Momma, now if you have something in your hand, you'll throw it. Momma, do you remember smashing all of our pictures? Glass went flying everywhere. You said you were sick of us, sick of everything."

Momma had been standing near the kitchen sink, still holding the glass of water in her hand; she still had tears in her eyes, but she seemed to be in a state of shock. She slowly put the glass in the sink, walked over to the table, sat down and dropped her head. "Momma, are you all right?" I asked. She only sat quietly and hung her head. My heart was beating so hard and fast that I thought I could almost hear it thumping. As Momma sat in the chair, she looked almost like a little girl who was being chastised by one of her parents. Had I talked too much? Why was she not saying anything? I kept talking; I had to for all of our sakes. I looked at Mom and said, "Momma, we love you more than anything in this world. All we ask, Momma, is that you get some help before you hurt yourself or one of us. Willie has a knot on his head from the fight that you and Randle had a few weeks ago. Somehow the whiskey bottle that you threw at Randle hit Willie in the face. It missed his eye by only a few inches, and he was lucky it didn't shatter in his face. Carmen has started to pull her hair out and bite her fingernails until they bleed. She's having nightmares that cause her to wake up screaming almost every night. You know this to be true, Momma—you've seen the fear in all of their eyes," I said.

Momma looked up at me from the table and extended her arms. From the look on her face she was really hurting. Had the realization of her actions finally sunk in? Please, Momma, I thought to myself, don't deny what's going on with you or us. I immediately fell into her arms and hugged her as tightly as I could, I felt like I was three years old again. Momma broke down crying on my shoulder and I cried like a baby; it was a very emotional moment for us. The close bond I felt with my mother during this time was beautiful; as we clung to each other, time seemed to stand still.

Momma finally began to speak. Her first words were, "Jessie, I am so sorry for what I've put you and the other children through. Please forgive me. I'm dealing with something that I thought I had put away in the past.

LeNora Millen

I know you don't know what I'm talking about, but maybe one day you'll understand. I'm trying to get my life together because I have become a complete failure in everything and by denying the problems that I've caused has only made the situation much worse. Most of all I didn't want to admit to my drinking problem. It's sad to say, but I've denied ever being an alcoholic. Even when the doctors told me I tried to tune them out. It took hearing all those horrible things that I've done, from you, to bring me to my senses. I thought that things would get better, but they've only gotten worse. Son, I know I need help and I promise you that I'll get it. I contacted a treatment center just this morning, but I froze up on the telephone. When the lady asked me my name, I hung up in her face. I thought that maybe I could deal with my own problems without an outsider's help, but you've helped me to take that first step. I want you to know that I was once told that no man would ever respect me until I respected myself first. When these words were spoke to me years ago, I spit at the person who spoke them, but the words have come back to haunt me. As I looked at myself in the mirror this morning, I didn't like the reflection staring back at me; I don't even look like the same woman to myself. I realize that Randle is one of my biggest problems. He's like a thorn in my side, and my life has taken a turn for the worse ever since he's entered it. For some reason, I keep picking the same type losers, who call themselves men. No more. I'm tired of the drinking, I'm tired of the profanities; I'm playing a game of Russian roulette with my life. The alcohol has really taken a toll on me and the beatings at the hands of Randle are just as bad. You don't know this, Jessie, but Randle would beat me at times if I refused to drink with him. He had enough nerves to call me his 'drinking buddy' and sometimes his 'drinking tramp.' Does this sound like a man talking, to you? My reward for refusal was his beatings. Our last fight was because of this. He is a crazy man, and I feel it's best for me to stay away from him before something drastic happens."

"He threatened to kill me the other night because I found out he was on crack and told him that I was going to call the police. I only said this to frighten him; he took it seriously. He put a gun to my face and said he'd blow me away without even thinking about it; and by the wild look on his face, I knew he meant it. I didn't think I was going to live to see any of you again."

I reminded Momma of when I had tried to warn her about seeing Randle come out of a crack house, and was cussed out and told to stay out of her business. Mom looked at me and said, "That was the whiskey talking, son. I know you didn't mean any harm. I've told Randle that it's over, but he's not accepting this. He seems to think that he's still able to walk back into my life. His confused mind seems to think that he owns me. Please try to understand that in order for me to get help I don't need him around, I don't even love the man, and, frankly, he doesn't love me. He's in love with the thought of having a woman he can slap around and tell what to do. He's a crack-head ,son, I can't deny this any longer. I don't want him around any of us, anymore; it's too dangerous."

I was happy to see that Momma was going to finally get help, but I was now dealing with the fear of Randle trying to come back into our lives; somehow I knew that this man was not going to let Momma go that easily.

Movement in the living room suddenly interrupted our talk; Carmen woke up crying and asking for Momma. Before I left the room, I reminded Momma of the envelope on the table that Mr. Moore had sent home. She said she would read it as soon as Carmen ate her soup. Tuesday morning rolled around and I was up before six o'clock that morning. I didn't get much sleep the night before, so much was on my mind—especially the talk Momma and I had. I couldn't recall when she had ever let go of her feelings like she had with me yesterday. I knew that the road ahead would be difficult for her, and I prayed that she wouldn't give up or give in when she felt she couldn't go on.

I called out to see whether Momma was up yet—she had an eight o'clock appointment with Mr. Moore at school today, and I wanted to make sure she wasn't late for it. I was relieved that Momma was already in the shower. She yelled out of the bathroom for me to wake Carmen and get her dressed.

Since Carmen had the measles, Momma was going to leave her with the neighbor all the kids in the neighborhood called "Mama Rose." Mama Rose was so kind and always called Carmen her little muffin when she saw her. She took such a liking to Carmen. I think it was because she never had any grandchildren of her own, and Carmen was the only little girl on our street. For whatever reason, she was always there to watch us whenever Momma was sober enough to take Carmen to her house, otherwise I had to baby-sit. Once we got to school, and checked in the principal's office, we were told to report to our scheduled class. I could not concentrate on my schoolwork because my mind was on Momma. I wondered how her appointment was going with Mr. Moore, and whether she was going to tell him the real reason we skipped school. So many questions were racing through my mind. I knew that Mr. Moore would do what he could to help us to get our lives in order and I knew that Momma wanted this, too. Today seemed like the longest school day ever; I couldn't stop watching the clock. This day of all days seemed to drag on forever.

After school, Willie, Aaron, and I raced home. We were so happy that Momma would be there. I had already told them about the talk Momma and I had, so they knew that Momma wanted to get help. I explained as best that I could, how we had to be there to help Momma whenever she needed us, because her getting better would not happen overnight. Momma was going to need our love and support more now than ever. I'd read about alcoholism, and knew that this was a disease and for the rest of Mom's life it would be a struggle for her. The cure for this disease was not to drink again, not even a sip.

When we got home from school, Momma was washing clothes. She realized we were home and said she needed to talk to all of us later. Mom told us that Mr. Moore had given her the name of one of his friends, who worked at a local treatment facility for alcoholism, and also the names of several family counselors that he knew. She explained to us that she had been honest with Mr. Moore about her problem, because she was tired of the lifestyle she was living, and knew that she had come close to having all of us taken away from her. Mr. Moore also told Momma that he would recommend family counseling for us because it was easy for him to determine that our behavior was associated with some type of dysfunction that we couldn't deal with. Momma wanted all of us to know that she would be going to treatment center as soon as possible. She gave all of us a big hug and told us to hang in there with her, because she loved us even though she had been very difficult to be around.

My 15th birthday was that Friday. I didn't have a birthday party, but I had the best present a son could ever ask for—my mother at home with the rest of us. Willie, Aaron and Carmen made me a birthday card; Momma baked me a chocolate cake and made hamburgers. Money was sparse, but we made it somehow. We had a lot of leftovers, and plenty of beans and cornbread. Patrick came over later that evening with a present he and his parents wanted me to have. According to Patrick it could change my whole life. I quickly tore through the gift-wrap; I couldn't believe my eyes. A leather-bound Bible with my name embossed on it in big letters: "Jessie Fremont." As I looked at my present, I felt overwhelmed. Tears suddenly welled up in my eyes—my very own Bible, with my name on it. All I could do was stare and smile.

I stood there a few minutes without saying anything, Patrick finally said, "What's wrong, Jessie? Cat got your tongue? Or do you have the holy ghost? Don't get to shouting on me, boy. If you faint, your mouth is so big I may fall in it trying to give you mouth-to-mouth. In your case, it's mouth of the south." We both burst out laughing.

I thanked Patrick for the gift he and his parents had given me. I told him to be sure and give his mother a kiss for me, and shake his pop's hand, "I ain't kissing no hairy-chest man," I said. Holding my Bible with my name on it made me feel important, like I was a preacher or something. I can't explain it, but when Patrick gave me that Bible a feeling of hope filled my body; it seemed like it came at just the right time. I ran into Mom's bedroom to show her my present. She looked briefly at it and said it was a nice gift, but she had the strangest expression on her face. Something bothered her about my gift; it was obvious that she felt uncomfortable with me receiving a Bible. It was not imagination. Patrick wanted me to attend church with him Sunday, so I asked Momma whether it would be okay with her since I had to baby-sit the last time. Momma said I could go, but she seemed uncomfortable in giving me her permission, for some whatever unexplained reason, whenever something came up about religion, or the church, Mom's attitude would change, but why?

Sunday morning greeted me with beautiful sunshine and birds chirping outside my window. I was finally going to church, Patrick's parents were honking the horn for me outside, so I had to rush out of the house. I ran out of door, still combing my hair. It seemed like I couldn't get in their car quick enough.

After speaking to everyone, I opened my Bible and read it until we reached Patrick's church. I had never been to a church before so today was very special day for me. As we entered his church, I felt afraid and out of place. I noticed how everyone shook hands; some of the people would hug or kiss each other. Everyone introduced themselves as brother or sister so-and-so. Patrick explained to me that since we're all God's children, we're sisters and brothers in Christ, because we are a part of God's family, I saw and felt so much love in those people that morning. I knew then that I wanted to be a part of God's family. I soon forgot that I was afraid, and I no longer felt like an outsider. Patrick's family introduced me to as many of their church members as they could.

When the congregation began singing, their voices blended in with complete harmony. Never had I heard singing sound so beautiful. I didn't know any of the songs. Patrick handed me a songbook, and I joined in. God knows I can't sing, but I did the best I could. Soon afterwards, the minister approached the pulpit. A hush fell upon the church. As the minister opened his Bible I looked at the faces of the church members—you could see the love and respect in their eyes as they gazed upon him. When he began to speak, I sat motionless and held on to every word he spoke. He preached about love. He said, "A lot of people walk around professing to know and love God, yet these same individuals are murdering our children with drugs, by flashing blood money in their face, they're gunning our youth down in the streets over something as petty as a dollar in a craps game." He went on. "They are robbing and assaulting our society with everything mentionable, from lack of education, to educating themselves to a life of crime, by way of drugs, to gangbanging… you name it. God is not in their hearts; if he was, a lot of the confusion mixed with hatred would stop. The killings would stop. God is love and if you say you love my father, and ignore his commandments, you're headed down a bottomless pit with no way out. How can you say you love God and disrespect your sister or brother? You disrespect God's children? You are serving the wrong master and it's definitely not my father in Heaven. I hear so many of our youth bragging about selling drugs. They say, "Why should I waste my time working a minimum-wage job when I can make more money in a day than the man sitting behind his big fancy desk can in a month? They soon drop out of school; they feel they don't need an education; they don't need college. They'll graduate by selling drugs; their diploma is only temporary, and their degree is only temporary. Oh, yes, they will get their reward, but it won't come from my Lord, it will come from their drug lord."

"God is our navigator," he said, "and he won't steer us in the wrong direction. Satan is the navigator of their ship, and the ship is sinking in sin. Our reward from the heavenly father is eternal life if we keep his commandments. Their reward is death, by way of sin, drive-by shootings, drug sales gone bad, drug overdoses—I could go on and on. While my father is saying, "Job well done," Satan is not satisfied. He says society needs to be shaken up some more, and he won't be satisfied until he can get to the innocent minds of God's children. Satan wants to infest and destroy their minds by way of his messengers of doom."

"Parents, we have to protect and watch over our children as the shepherd watches over his flock. When one of our children goes astray, or gets lost in the world, we have to go after him, keeping in mind that our heavenly father is always watching over his children. And he won't let his sheep get too far before he'll snatch them back. Your faith in our father is what holds the family together. The task won't be easy because of what our little ones are confronted with each day. Instead of tempting a child with a piece of candy, they're tempted with a piece of crack."

The minister's voice shouted across the room, as the speakers vibrated his godly plea, "Church, we have to keep praying, because we cannot fight against Satan without God. We have to put on the whole armor of God, because we cannot fight this battle alone."

After he finished his sermon, such an intense feeling came over me. I wasn't sure, but I thought I had been filled with what I heard Patrick so often refer to as the Holy Ghost. At that very moment I wanted to do his will, and I wanted to be baptized. Most importantly, I wanted my family to be there with me when it happened. Oh, God, I thought, what if all of us got baptized at the same time? I know all the angels in Heaven would rejoice! If only Momma and the others could have been at church today to hear the sermon. I know she would have felt differently about church, but would she really have?

I noticed that everyone was in the church aisles laughing and talking with one another. My mind was full and I didn't want to forget anything that I had heard during the sermon. I looked across the church for Patrick and saw him standing at the back of the church with his Mom and Dad; they were talking to the minister. I had made my mind up that I wanted to be baptized, and I wanted Patrick to hear the good news, I knew I had to get Mom's approval first, though, but why was I so afraid? Surely she would say yes; at least, I hoped she would.

CHAPTER 3

I met Patrick and his family at the front of the church; I got a chance to shake the minister's hand after introducing myself. I told him how much I enjoyed his sermon. He smiled as he held my hand, and said that he was glad that I got some meat, and he hoped that he had fed me enough, because he wanted me to leave God's house full. He also reminded me that I should always thirst after righteousness. While speaking to me he looked directly in my eyes, almost as if he could see something behind my pupils, then said, "Come back again, son, because it's not safe out on the streets. I remember how it was when I came up; it was bad then, it's worse now. We need God's protection more now than ever."

I again thanked the minister and promised him that I would visit him again; somehow, in my heart, I knew I would. We all said our goodbyes before leaving church.

On the way home Patrick's parents asked me whether I enjoyed the worship service. From the excitement in my voice, it was easy for them to see that I had. Patrick was sitting next to me in the back seat; he kept nudging me and said, "Let me tell them, Jessie. Man, let Rev. Slick tell them."

Patrick's mother said, "Tell us what? Because if that boy says let me tell them one more time, I'm gonna stick his dad's sock in his mouth!" She looked at Patrick and said, "Son, how many times have I told you that Rev. Slick got replaced with Rev. Do Right?" Patrick seemed to ignore her comment. Patrick was a regular goofball when he wanted to be. He couldn't move his lips fast enough in telling his parents that I had decided to be baptized and become a member of their church. They were both pleased and commended me for wanting to do God's will. Patrick's dad asked me whether I had made my own mind up in my decision to come to the lord through baptism, because he didn't want Patrick or anyone else to force me to be baptized, or to force me to attend church. At first I didn't understand what would have been wrong with someone forcing me to go to church. At least I would be there. Pop explained to me that this would not be the proper way to glorify God; he said that it had to be my own decision, and my heart should be right first.

I quickly responded by telling Pop that I had been wanting to learn as much as I could about baptism. "Patrick has explained God and baptism to me the best he could, and suggested that I talk to you and his minister if I had any questions. Why do you think I asked you so many questions about being baptized the last time was over to your house, Pop? What you told me helped me to better understand God's commandments. My mind was made up then, and after hearing today's sermon only made me want it more."

Pop smiled and said, "That's good, and we're very proud of you for making your own mind up. How does your mother feel about it, Jessie?"

I swallowed hard, but I answered honestly, "She doesn't know yet, Pop, but as soon as I get home and see that she is not too busy, I'll talk to her about it, because I want her and the rest of my family to be there when I'm baptized. I'm praying I'll be an example for them and that they will soon come to the Lord, too."

Pop gave me a big smile, then Patrick's mom said she wanted me to know that she had a lot of confidence in me and she could see that I was going to make my family very proud of me one day. She said she was pleased with me taking religion so seriously, but she wanted me to be aware that, on occasion, there would be conflicts in the church as there are conflicts outside of the church. When this happens in the family of God, He is not pleased, and we need to learn to pray about these things and not hold grudges. She went on to tell me about a group of young men in the church who had gone on a camping trip, respectable young men, handworkers in the church, she said. According to Patrick's mom these young men decided to play a joke on one of the boys in the group who they considered Mr. Goody Two Shoes. When he fell asleep that night, they got a hold of his duffel bag, found his clothes, and sprinkled itching powder all over them. That wasn't enough for them—they also put deep heat in his boxer shorts. Naturally when they got up to dress the next morning for their hike through the woods, this young man came flying through the trees toward everyone in sight, tearing his clothes off, and screaming about his butt feeling like it was on fire. They tell me that clothes were flying everywhere. The boys were laughing uncontrollably, seeing Mr. Goody Two Shoes do an unrehearsed strip-tease show. I was told that when he got down to his boxer shorts he practically tore them off and headed as fast as his feet could take him in the direction of the lake and jumped in it, in a squatting position.

In order for the young men to protect their wrong-doing it was said that the young man wanted some attention, so he decided to rip his clothes off and moon one of the deacons at the church. The truth finally surfaced when the conscience of one of the boys involved in the joke wouldn't let him rest with the lie. He knew what they had done was wrong even though it was meant to be only a harmless prank. The elders reprimanded each of the young men. They also had to personally apologize to the young man. The incident was so embarrassing to the young man that he had decided to attend another church. Had it not been for the love and support from the church, he and his family may have changed their membership.

All of a sudden, Patrick said, "Now I know what it means to be the butt of the joke." I tried to hold back my laughter, but I couldn't—even Mrs. Munson was laughing.

Patrick and I were curious to know who the young man was, since she never mentioned his name. We figured she must not have known. She seemed hesitant in telling us who he was at first, then she said, "I'll give you a clue. Had this young man left the church, he would have left part of his future behind."

Patrick and I looked at each other, we could not figure out what she was talking about. Her second clue was, "This person is quite familiar with you, Jessie; and Patrick knows him all too well." Finally, she said, "Had this young man left the church, one of you would not be riding in the back seat of the car this morning."

We both knew the answer instantly. I yelled out "Pop." Patrick was hysterically laughing and yelling "Dad, it was you. I can't believe it, oh no, my dad, you were the Mr. Goody Two-Shoes, I can't believe it, Dad?" Patrick couldn't stop laughing.

Pop only smiled and said, "If you keep laughing, son, you're going to be the butt of my belt. As for your mother, she's never been one to keep a secret."

I couldn't remember when I'd had so much fun. Afterwards I thanked Mrs. Munson for being honest with me about what I might encounter as a Christian. She said her only reason for telling me these things was not to discourage me, but to enlighten or prepare me for it when and if it happened. She also told me that, as a Christian, I was to be just as humble and kind to those not in the church. She went on to say that sometimes lost souls are won by shining our light wherever we go in a positive way, and when we see our light growing dim; we are to work on what is causing our Christian light to flicker, and not shine as brightly. "We must learn to work on the area or areas that cause our light to dim," she said, "and by renewing our faith, in a sense, when we begin to grow weak. As adults we should not paint pretty pictures about life to our children, because life is no fairytale and we're dealing with the real world. Jessie, you are the backbone of our future. You were born into a society that is ready to offer you all that's in it, good and bad; it's left up to you to make the right choice. You hold the key to your future; God holds the master key. Never forget this—always put God first. Strive to be the best in whatever your goals may be. You've heard that old saying that a woman's work is never done? Well, I'm here to tell you that a Christian's work is never done. I hope you know that I'm telling you these things, Jessie, because I love you like a son. So does Pop. Patrick has already heard these same words spoken to him, haven't you, son?"

"Yes, ma'am," Patrick replied, "and a lot more. Once Momma gets cranked up, she'll talk until she runs out of things to say. But seriously, Jessie, I love her and Pop for being here for me when I need them, because sometimes I really get scared when I think about what would happen to me if I didn't have Momma or Pop around. From what I've seen happen to some of our friends, how they're gunned down in the streets for saying something smart, or just making fun of each other, or being just an innocent bystander, it makes me wonder whether any of them really care about life, even their own. They don't even think twice about being locked behind bars. I used to think I was better than they were. Especially some of the kids at school who were always causing problems. It wasn't hard to spot the one's who sold drugs, or was on suspension. By a twist of fate, I got a chance to talk to one of them. I was scared at first because I knew it didn't take much to get knocked into a locker when it came to him. His temper would go off like a stick of dynamite with a short fuse."

"Who are you talking about, Patrick?" I asked.

Patrick's tone took on a more serious tone as he said, "You know, Jessie, the boy everybody at school called 'Nitty,' short for Frank Nitty."

I was shocked. I didn't even know Patrick had enough nerve to talk to this guy; he was right on the verge of being crazy. If you smiled the wrong way at him, you were asking to be knocked into a concrete wall—even worse, beaten silly for no apparent reason outside of just looking at him the wrong way. Nitty enjoyed being glamorized as the tough guy. He felt sort of like he was a celebrity—always full of anger and drama, he seemed to feast off of his own hatred.

Patrick seemed to gather his thoughts as spoke about the day he had run into Nitty. He said, "Jessie, you and I both know that everyone is afraid of Nitty, even some the teachers at school. They would give him a suspension rather than confront him. When I saw him I would go in the opposite direction. I would see him and his protégés who hung with him. They were so afraid of him that, as a pawn to keep from being beaten up, they would join his gang." Patrick told us about the day he happened to walk in the boys' bathroom during lunch and saw Nitty leaning up against the bathroom wall with a worried look on his face.

"I stopped dead in my tracks," he said. "I remember looking around to see whether any of his sidekicks were there. I knew what I would have been up against had they been there. Talk about being scared, I almost wet my pants before I got through the bathroom door. I spoke to Nitty and held my breath because I didn't know what he had on his mind, and I didn't want to be his next victim. He didn't speak—he just looked at me. I asked him whether he was all right because he looked like he had been crying. He only frowned, looking at me under-eyed, and said, 'What's it to you, man? Like your phony little butt really cares.'"

"'I do care,' I said. 'You look like you don't feel well. You aren't sick, are you?'"

"Nitty yelled to the top of his voice—echoes of his voice penetrating the bathroom stalls still make me shudder. He yelled, 'Hell, naw, I ain't sick, but if you don't get your Bible–totin' butt out of here and leave me alone, somebody's gonna walk in here and find you stuffed in that toilet over there, you little smart-mouth wimp.'"

"I backed off and said, 'Okay, I didn't mean any harm. I was just worried about you. Man, there are some people in this world who care about helping people. I might be afraid of you, but I wouldn't want anything happening to you.'"

"He gave me the meanest look, then he pointed his finger at me and said, 'You've got three seconds to get out of here, choir-boy—three seconds.'"

"I got out there as fast as I could. About two weeks later, I was walking home from school and saw about four or five guys fighting. Turns out it was the gang across town. They were all taking turns hitting someone—whoever it was he didn't seem to be fighting back, probably because they were too weak. I hid behind the bushes next to Mr. Charlie's store. I knew I would be their next victim if they spotted me. I looked across the street through the bushes. I could see the neighbors peeping out of their windows. Why don't they call the police? Then I thought maybe they have. I kept peeping through the bushes so I could see who it was in the street. I could also hear police sirens getting closer. I heard one of them yell out,

SEEDS OF DECEPTION

'Let's go, man.' I immediately ran from behind the bushes to help whoever it was. As I got closer I was shocked to see that it was Nitty. He was beat up pretty bad and as I stared at him, I couldn't help but to feel sorry for him. He looked so pitiful and helpless, I took my coat off, covered him with it, and placed his head on my lap. He was slipping in and out of consciousness. I was relieved to see an ambulance headed toward us; there were police cars everywhere. They put him on a stretcher and placed him in the ambulance. He was covered in blood, and it looked like his nose was smashed in, too."

"The only information I could give the police was what I had seen when I got there. I don't know what the neighbors saw. They were asking about relatives or next of kin. I couldn't tell them anything. An old lady from the crowd stepped forward to tell the police, that she was the one who had called them. She said, for fear of her life, she and the other neighbors were afraid to come out of their homes because these gang members had threatened them on many occasions. She told the police that Nitty lived with his sister and they would have to contact her, because his parents had been killed in an accident years ago."

Patrick's mother interrupted him and said, "I will never forget that evening Patrick came home; I thought I was going to have a heart attack when he came walking through the door with blood all over his clothes. I started screaming and wanted to know what had happened to him. I didn't know whether he had been stabbed, shot or what was wrong. After my nerves finally settled down, he explained to me what had happened. I was proud that Patrick was brave enough to stay and help the young man until the ambulance arrived, but Jessie, I want you to know that your buddy didn't get any sleep that night. He said every time he closed his eyes, he could see Nitty's beat-up face. We all said a prayer for him and his family and prayed for his speedy recovery."

Patrick said that Mr. Charlie told him that Nitty's parents had been killed in an accident when he was ten years old. Nitty's sister had custody of him, but he felt like she couldn't tell him what to do. Patrick said that Mr. Charlie told him that Nitty's sister said she once told him that her brother hadn't been right since their parents had died. She said he cried a lot and stayed angry all the time. He once told her that she wasn't his mother and not to try to order him around. He said when their parents were living they could tell him what to do; no one else could, and he wasn't taking orders from anybody. Mr. Charlie said he sometimes let her have food on credit, and that Nitty's sister had come into his store crying because her brother would steal most her money, and tried to fight her once because she had confronted him about it.

I looked at Patrick's mom and told her about an incident that I encountered with Nitty and his gang. Mrs. Munson wanted to know more. I described how I had gone in Mr. Charlie's store one Saturday, described how Mr. Charlie had to call the police on Nitty because he had come into his store with his gang and tried to pick a fight with two other boys. They were so afraid of him that they gave their money away, which wasn't good enough for Nitty—he said one of the boys had stepped on his new tennis shoes, and he wanted the boy to lick the spot clean. His gang was laughing and started slapping the boys upside their heads. Mr. Charlie offered Nitty a towel and some cleanser to clean the shoe. Nitty started cussing, then pointed his finger in Mr. Charlie's face and said, "Old man, if you want to see your false teeth grinning back at you in the mirror, you'd better get back behind that counter." Mr. Charlie stepped behind the counter and dialed 911 before Nitty saw him. Nitty was too busy running his mouth and keeping up confusion.

I was on the other side of the store while all of this was happening, too scared to move. In my mind I kept saying, why don't those police hurry up and get here before one of those maniacs sees me. As soon as that thought left my mind, one of the gang members, Hambone, 250 pounds and all, came down the aisle toward me. I didn't even have time to hide before he spotted me and yelled out, "Hey Nitty, look what I found hanging out behind the can goods." I knew I could out-run him. I took off running in the opposite direction, Hambone, with his fat butt, slipped and knocked can goods all across the floor. By the time I had made it toward the front of the store, I could hear the police sirens. I can't remember when I've ever been so glad to see the police. Nitty and his gang were hauled off in handcuffs after Mr. Charlie gave his police report. I stayed and helped him put everything back in place.

While we were cleaning the store, Mr. Charlie said that Nitty had been in juvenile detention so much that it didn't bother him to go back, because he knew that he'd be getting right out after he's stayed a few weeks or months. Mr. Charlie said he had known Nitty's parents before they were killed in the accident and told me that they were such a nice couple. He said he had watched Nitty and his sister Joyce grow up in the neighborhood. His sister only wanted the best for her brother, yet Nitty gave up hope once his parents died. Mr. Charlie just shook his head and said, "I wish there was something I could have done to make things better for them, but Nitty chooses to travel his own self-destructive road. His sister usually has him taken in when he tries to fight her, or stays out all times of the night. All I can say is that if Nitty keeps going in the direction that he's headed, he won't live to see his 16th birthday."

"He's right, Jessie," Patrick said. "That's why I found myself feeling so sorry for him. I realized that I was blessed enough to have parents living; he doesn't. He seems to be crying out for help, but no one really understands. The school deals with him by kicking him out, they suspend him, when people on the street see him, they see trouble; their solution is to run and hide or lock their doors."

Pop gave let out a big sigh and said, "Son, maybe we need to start opening our minds and hearts and begin to reach out, instead of turning our back on the problem, or trying to put the problem on someone else's doorstep. Until we start to face our problems, by getting to the core of them, rather than running from the problems, this madness will continue. Until man starts to change his selfish ways, society will remain the same. Our youth on the streets and our youth locked away will always remain society's stepchildren."

Pop was definitely a man of wisdom; I only hoped something good would come out of my generation. As we approached my house that morning's sermon was still fresh on my mind. After I got of the car I thanked Patrick's parents for giving me a ride to and from church. I told them how much I enjoyed the long talk we had, I said goodbye to everyone, and watched them pull off in the car. As I stood on the sidewalk and looked up at the house, somehow it looked different. I used to hate coming home, but now coming home felt different, since Mom had decided to get help for her drinking problem—it had given my entire family a since of hope. I even appreciated life more; this old house was once a shell to me, now it felt like home. As I stood in front of the house, with my Bible clutched under my arm, I began to feel joy rush through my body; I suddenly raced up the stairs leading to the front door. I unlocked the door and called out for Mom; she was on the living room couch, combing Carmen's hair, Willie and Aaron were on the floor watching television. "Hey everybody, I can't wait to tell y'all about church today."

Everybody spoke at same time, "Jessie tell us about church," Aaron yelled at the top of his voice. Mom looked at me a said, "Jessie, you look mighty happy about something; still excited?"

Sort of blushing, I replied, "Yes, ma'am, and you could make me even happier."

"Oh, really," Momma replied.

"Yes, ma'am," I said. "I've got to talk to you about something when you have time; it's very important." I went in the bedroom and got out of my church clothes.

Willie and Aaron came into the room while I was undressing; they wanted me to tell them all about what happened at church, "Did you shout, Jessie?" Willie asked.

I laughed and said, "Naw, Willie. I didn't shout, but I did sing."

"You sang?" he said. "I know everybody was crying at that church, 'cause you sound like you're in pain when you sing." Willie always had something smart to say.

I told them that next time I wanted all of them to come to church with me, because I had decided to get baptized, "But first I'm going to have to talk with Momma about it, so let's keep it a secret until I get her permission."

Aaron and Willie wanted to know what it meant to be baptized, and was it like taking a shower. Aaron asked if the soul was being cleansed, how come they didn't use any soap? I was glad I could explain it to them; it wasn't too long ago that I was asking questions about baptism.

After I explained everything I could to them, they were frowning, Aaron said it sounded weird. I told them when they got a little older, they would understand it better.

During dinner Momma told us that she would begin her treatment for her drinking problem in a week, and we would have to stay with Mama Rose while she was there—she didn't want us to be at the house by ourselves. Mom told us that she would be in a support group with others who were going through almost the same thing she was, so she felt good about knowing that she could openly discuss her drinking problems, and not be embarrassed by it. She looked at me and said, "Jessie, I want you to know that Mr. Moore said he would take the time out of his schedule and drive me to the meetings. He is such a nice man and I really appreciate how he has helped me to try to get my life back on track." She smiled and said, "His support means a lot; I don't think I would have had the nerves to go through this without his encouragement."

I smiled, because I was thinking to myself since Mr. Moore was single and Momma was single, how nice it would be if he and Momma started seeing each other. She deserved some happiness because she had been hurt so much by Randle and some of the other deadbeats she had dated in the past.

Momma told all of us that we would start family counseling as soon as she was making progress with her treatment. Aaron asked Momma whether she would have to take any shots for her problem. Gently rubbing Aaron across the head, Mom answered in a reassuring way, "No, I won't have to take any shots, Aaron—the only way any alcoholic gets better is with self-discipline and staying away from any alcoholic beverage."

Mom's answer seemed to have put Aaron at ease. He smiled and said, "I'm glad you don't have to take any shots, Momma, cause I hate those big needles, I'd rather take a children's aspirin."

Willie seemed somewhat annoyed with Aaron and said, "Stop asking so many questions, Aaron. Hurry up and eat your food so we can go outside and play ball." Willie looked at Mom and said, "Momma, you're gonna be fine; I know you will."

His encouraging words even gave me hope. Focusing her attention on me, Momma asked me what I needed to talk with her about. I told her I would tell her all about it after dinner. "Why can't you tell me now?" she asked.

I winked at Mom and jokingly said, "Because this food is so good, Momma, that I can't really concentrate on anything else; I'll talk to you about it after dinner." Momma gave me one of those, "yeah, sure, Jessie" looks.

Willie and Aaron were smiling at me and elbowing each other. "Stop clowning at the table, you two," Momma snapped. "Why are you grinning at Jessie, anyway?"

Willie blurted out, "It's a secret, Momma."

By that time Momma got up from the table to put her plate in the sink. I told her I would wash the dishes and clean the kitchen up for her; she could go on and watch television and get some rest.

Mom looked at me and said, "I don't know what you're trying to butter me up for, Jessie; if it's something new, you know I don't have the money right now."

"Oh, Momma," I said, "I'm not trying to butter you up. I'm just trying to be helpful because you cooked such a good dinner. I can't remember when we've had turkey and dressing and cranberry sauce! Go ahead, Momma, and relax. I told you I'd wash the dishes." I thought to myself, Mom's right, I really was up to something. I knew I had to be careful the way I approached Momma with anything related to religion, but why? I knew that this was something that Mom had trouble dealing with, and I didn't want to ask her when she was already upset about something. I knew as long as her mind was relaxed and her nerves were calm, I might have a better chance.

I had to rehearse how I was going to ask her. "Momma, I want to get baptized." No, that's too forceful. "Momma, I feel like I'm ready to go to the Lord." No, that's sounds like I'm dying or something. How will I approach her? Hopefully by the time I got through cleaning the kitchen, I'd know exactly how to ask her. "Please, God, help me," I prayed. "Please put the right words in my mouth. With your guidance, from what Patrick says, I'll know exactly what to say and how to say it."

I peeped out of the kitchen to see where Momma was. "Good," I thought. She had taken my advice and was on the couch watching television. I only had a few more dishes to wash and was still rehearsing in my mind on how I would tell Mom about my decision in wanting to be baptized. I knew Mom was just as curious to know what I wanted to ask her as I was in knowing what her answer would be. "I don't know why I'm so worried about her saying no. Maybe I need to think positive and have faith in believing that everything is going to be all right."

I could hear Mom laughing; something funny must have been on television. Whatever it was, it didn't matter, as long as she was beginning to feel better, and starting to smile more. I'd heard that laughter was good for the soul. In Mom's case, it was just what she needed. Thank God for giving her enough courage to finally get help for herself. By her having us to support her, I think this made her stronger in her will to get counseling.

My thoughts were interrupted by a knock at the door. I yelled out to Mom that I would get it. When I opened the door, my mind went blank. I couldn't believe it, of all people—Randle. Oh no, I thought, not today of all days, why did you have to show up? Before I knew it, I called out his name. He arrogantly replied, "That's my name. You got a problem or something, boy?" I just looked at him, looking wild in the eyes, he yelled, "Let me in. You act like you're crazy or something. Standing with your mouth wide open, like you're hungry. Where's your Mom? I need to get something straight with her." I was still holding the door halfway open. I knew Mom was on the couch and I didn't want Randle to see her. Mom had already told me that she was afraid of him, and wasn't going to see him anymore.

"She's asleep, Randle, and she told us not to let you in here anymore. Mom's afraid of you, and she's trying to get help for herself."

Looking as if he was ready to sucker-punch me, he said, "Boy, what are you talking about? Your Mom don't have any reason to be scared of me; I don't know what she's been telling y'all, but I'm going to find out. Now let me in. You scared, too?"

Still holding the doorknob, I said, "Naw, I ain't scared. I've seen uglier people than you before."

Randle frowned and said, "Say what, boy? I'll smack your smart mouth crooked. I'm sick of you anyway. Don't you think I haven't noticed how you roll them big eyes at me when I come over? I told your Momma long time ago that you don't need a butt-whipping, you need a beating." Drool could be seen forming at the corners of his mouth. He smelled like urine and looked as if he hadn't bathed in weeks. He pointed his finger in my face and said, "You see, I don't care if you don't like me, because I don't come here to see you, anyway. You're like a roach to me, I could squash you without thinking twice."

While Randle was rambling off, Mom had eased off of the couch and crawled across the floor to the bedroom, before he spotted her. I was scared, but found the courage to do what I could to protect my mother. Randle's eyes looked like they were rolling to the top of his head. Sweat was popping out all over his face. It was obvious that he was drunk or high on something. He was talking loud and telling Mom that she had better stop dodging him, and that if she knew what was good for her, she'd talk to him. Mom tipped out of the bedroom with the broom in her hand. She looked at me and put her finger up to her mouth—my clue to keep my mouth shut. Randle still couldn't see her since she was standing up against wall behind the door. Oh, Mom, I thought, what are you going to do with that broom?

Randle was still yelling and pleading with her to talk to him. He started making threats on Mom's life, talking about how he'd wring her neck, and if she thought she was gonna turn her back on him—in a threatening tone he said he'd kill her first. He acted like a crazy man or something. To make matters worse, he tried to force his way into the house. With Randle physically drunk, my reflexes were quicker. I shoved the door back toward him.

Out of nowhere Mom jumped from behind me and swung at him with the broom. Randle started laughing and said, "Woman, you gone crazy.

Don't you know that if I wanted to I could take that broom from you and sweep you and your nappy-headed ass son across this whole house?"

Mom told Randle that before she'd let him hurt her again, or try to hurt any of us, she'd kill him first, because she was not taking any more of his abuse. She said, "If it means going to jail, I'll have to. I don't care." Randle had enough nerves to laugh again. He told Mom that she was the one who was crazy, and that she would never find anyone to treat her like he had. He was loud and sarcastic in his verbal attacks. He told her that she was making a fool out of herself if she thought she could find someone else.

Mom's facial expression was of anger and hurt. Tightening the belt on her robe, she replied angrily, "I'm making a fool out of myself if I stay with you. What have you ever done for me or my children, Randle? Nothing; the only thing you've done is to cause my children and me problems. Because of you I have become an alcoholic and abusive toward my children."

Randle, acting somewhat amused at Mom's questions, started laughing, then said, "Look at your Mom, boy, talking about how I've caused her to drink. She did it because she wanted to, and now she wants to put the blame on me. Standing up there with that broom in her hand like somebody's maid or something."

Mom started crying and screaming for him to get out of her life and stay out of it. She seemed almost out of control. She looked at Randle and said, "I'm not afraid to pop you across your mouth with this broom, so I would advise you to get away from my door right now."

Randle threw his arms up in the air, too drunk to walk, almost falling; he slowly backed away, and sarcastically said, "I'm not through with you, Betty; it ain't that simple." He mumbled something under his breath in my direction that I couldn't understand. Still stumbling and pointing in Mom's direction, he said, "You'd better pray like you pretend you don't know how to, because you're going to need it. No one talks to me like I'm a dog and gets away with it. You gonna need more than a broom next time."

Momma was shaking and crying hysterically. I tried desperately to calm her. It seemed as if she had tuned me out. I tried unsuccessfully to calm her; nothing seemed to work. I could only continue to hold her and tell her that everything would be all right. Mom started yelling for me to find the children and to bring them indoors before Randle saw them. Still hysterical, she began to scream, "Why did he have to show up? I didn't deserve this." I did what I could to calm her down. Before leaving, I told her to lock the door; she was not in any shape to go out. I knew that it wouldn't be a good idea, since Randle had just left. After making sure Mom was safely locked in; I went after my sister and brothers.

CHAPTER 4

Before I got halfway down the street, I heard Aaron calling my name. He was holding Carmen as he and Willie ran toward me. In a frantic voice Aaron told me that Randle had come to the park where they were. He said that Randle was cussing and saying bad things about Momma. Willie, still out of breath from running, said, "Jessie, he said he was going to hurt anybody who got in him and Mom's way." Willie said that Randle told them that he wasn't going to bother them; he said he just wanted him to give Momma this message—that it wasn't over, until he says it was over, then he walked away. Nervously, Willie asked whether Randle was telling the truth.

"Yeah, Willie," I said. "I'm afraid he was." I told them some of what had happened at the house, and how we would have to be careful even when we answered the door. Aaron yanked on the bottom of my shirt and said, "I'm scared, Jessie. What if Randle comes back again and tries to kill us?"

All I could say was, "Don't be scared; we'll take care of Momma." I was just as scared, but I didn't want them to know this. Oh God, I thought, please protect all of us and watch over Momma, and please keep Randle away from her.

As we walked home, my mind took me back to something Randle said to Momma. What did he mean by she had better pray like she pretended she didn't know how to! I remember Mom's expression on her face, a shocked look, as if she was reminded of something that she had wanted to forget. I didn't even know Momma ever prayed, or even thought about it. Was Momma keeping something from us about religion? It was strange that whenever the word "church" was mentioned, Momma would change the subject or get real quiet. What was it that Momma was hiding from us about church?

When we got home, we checked to see whether Momma had calmed down. She hadn't; she was a nervous wreck. She told us that she was going to have to get the locks changed on the doors, because she knew that Randle once had keys to the house. He said he had lost them, but to be on the safe side, she would change the locks, anyway. She told us that if we saw Randle on the street, to go the other way, and for all of us to walk home from school together, not to split up, because she didn't know what he had on his mind.

Willie told Mom what Randle had said. She looked scared and said that she was going down to the police department and file a restraining order against him, because he had threatened her too many times and it was time to take his threats seriously. Mom went on to say that she wouldn't be able to rest until Randle was locked up and she hoped that he would get treatment for his drinking and drug problem, because even if he was locked up and released he still would be an alcoholic and addicted to drugs. "He needs treatment and counseling, just like I do," she said, "and by seeing how abusive he acted toward me, this only made me to want to get help even more. I could see how mean and ugly a person can get, when their mind is not their own, but a drug-induced mind. I can't believe how I could have let this happen to me, and worst of all it caused me to be such a horrible person toward you all. What's so bad about what happened with Randle was that after he left and upset me, I started to thirst for a drink—not water, but alcohol—because I wanted to deal with him through getting drunk and trying to forget him. This is a struggle for me. I thought about you all and that helped me out some, I'm not saying it was easy, though, and I know that there will be other times that I will be tempted to drink. That's why I need the counseling so bad I realized that I can't go that route alone. I know that I couldn't even if I thought I could."

I asked Mom to stop blaming herself for how she had been acting, and reminded her that she was the most important person in our lives, and no matter how difficult things got, we would be there for her. All of us gave Mom a hug and kiss and told her that we loved her.

Willie and the others left the room to play games. Mom looked at me and said something to me that I will never forget, she said, "Jessie, I know that I've been very hard on you, and I have dumped so much on you. You've been like a father to your sister and brothers; you've helped me in so many ways. I want you to know that I'm thankful to have a son who is mature enough and unselfish enough to give love, even when he's not receiving it. I know that you have cried many tears because of me. Son, I've cried, too, not because I felt sorry for myself, but because I saw what I was doing to my children and for some unforeseen reason I couldn't control myself. I could see the hurt in all of your eyes, but I didn't know how to make the hurt better. Jessie, you are very special child. You remind me of someone I once knew. He was so patient, and he truly loved me. Never have I known or met another man like him. No matter how harsh I was to him, he seemed to always have a kind word for me. All he wanted to do was love and help me, and I was just too selfish to appreciate his unselfish love."

As Mom talked about this man, her eyes lit up. She appeared to almost go back in time as she batted her long eyelashes, smiled and said, "He was the love of my life." Curiosity got to me, and I asked Mom about this man. Mom only smiled and said, "Someone very special."

Seeming to snap back to reality Mom's expression changed to serious. She started stuttering as if she wanted to push back emotions of the past. I asked again, "Mom, are you sure you can't remember his name?" Appearing to be at a loss for words, she said, "I can't remember, son. If I think of it, I'll tell you." Mom had a habit of twisting her hair around her fingers when stressed or nervous. She had started to twist a strand of her long hair around her fingers. This was my cue to change the subject.

"Jessie," she said, "since the kids are playing in the room, now would be a good time to have that talk you mentioned earlier." I told Mom it could wait, because I didn't think it would be a good time to ask because of what had happened today. Mom smiled and said, "I'm all right now, Jessie. Go ahead."

I was speechless; I told Mom I didn't know where to start. I reminded her of Patrick and how he was a good friend of mine. She smiled and said, "you and Patrick should have been twins—always with each other."

"That's right, Mom," I said, "he is my best friend, and he's been good for me spiritually. He's really taught me a lot about God. Sometimes during our lunch hour at school he and I study and discuss the Bible together. Every now and then we get teased by some of the kids; we're called 'weirdoes' or the 'choirboys.' Most of the time we laugh at them or just ignore them. Hopefully one day, they will realize that without God, they're nothing. There's still a lot that I have to read and study about in the Bible, but the more I read, Mom, the more I need to understand what I'm reading about. Sometimes it gets real confusing, and I'll ask Patrick about what certain verses mean. If he doesn't understand, he usually will ask his dad or their minister. Mom, did you know that Patrick wants to preach God's word one day?"

Mom sort of frowned and said, "No, Jessie, I didn't know that, but the way he's been on you about going to church with him, I knew that he was really serious about religion."

"Yes, ma'am, he is. His religion is very important to him. Don't get me wrong, Mom, he's not a fanatic—just a good person. I've gotten serious about religion also, Mom, that's why I wanted to talk to you. Mom, I want to know whether I could start going to church with Patrick. I've also decided that I want to be baptized, but of course I need your approval first. Please, Mom, say yes."

Mom didn't say anything at first, she just looked at me. She had started to twist her hair around her fingers again. She sat quiet for a few seconds, and just stared, then said, "It's too soon for me to give you an answer. Let me think about it."

At least she didn't say no, I thought to myself. This gave me some hope. As I got up to leave the room, Mom asked me whether I had been praying or did I know how to pray.

I didn't answer her immediately because her question sort of caught me off-guard. "Yes, ma'am, I pray all the time," I answered. "I also have a prayer that Patrick's mother wrote for me, it's at school taped to the inside of my locker. I read it for encouragement when things get tough. I've been trying to memorize it, but I haven't been able to concentrate lately, I'll bring it home and let you read it. It's beautiful, Mom. When I first read it, I felt like crying—not because I was sad, but because it made me feel like I was special. Sometimes when I pray, I find myself saying the same thing over and over again, but I know that God knows what I'm trying to say. When I was praying for you, Mom, it looked like the words came out so easy. I know it is because of my love for you. I was crying out to God, and he heard my cry. Mom, I started to see a change in you. I know that prayer really does change things. My faith in God is so strong even though I'm still learning about this miraculous God through Patrick and his family. I know in my heart that our family is being blessed and I thank God everyday for giving you strength in dealing with alcoholism."

Mom sat still for a few minutes, then said, "Jessie, I know you mean well, and I know that you've found strength in your belief in God. I really need to get my head together before I can think clearly, so much has been happening lately and with Randle showing up, this just ruined my whole day."

Not really knowing the direction the conversation was headed I said, "Yes, ma'am, I understand, but I need to know whether I can go to church Sunday, even if you haven't made your mind up. I'll take Carmen, Willie, and Aaron with me this time. Patrick's parents won't mind. They asked about them other day, they wanted to know whether they could start coming to church with me."

Appearing somewhat concerned, and I guess feeling inadequate about Patrick's parents asking about her children, Mom said, "Son, let's take this one step at a time. I'm giving you my approval to go with Patrick and his family, but the children need to stay home, because they really don't have any nice church clothes." I tried to reassure Mom that their clothes were nice enough for them to wear, and that all they needed was a good starching and ironing. Mom quickly replied, "Jessie, I said no. I would feel better if they stayed at home, especially since Randle is on a rampage."

I didn't want to press the issue, so I said, "Fine, Mom, if that's what you want. But I do have a very important question to ask."

Mom looked puzzled and said, "What's that, son?"

I smiled and said, "Mom, if you give me permission to be baptized, I want all of you to be at church with me. Mom, would you please come? It would make me so happy. I wouldn't feel right if my family is not there with me, especially if you're not there."

I held my breath, because I didn't know what Mom was going to say. Surprisingly enough, she said, "Jessie, if I give you permission to be baptized, I will definitely be there, I promise."

Before I knew it, I'd jumped straight out of the chair into the air. I kept thanking Mom over and over. Willie, Aaron and Carmen came running out of the room wanting to know what I was so excited about, I told them that Mom was letting me go back to church Sunday, and she said she would think about me getting baptized. Willie and Aaron did what they called a victory dance, and Carmen was jumping up and down, clapping her hands.

Mom got up off the couch, shaking her head laughing. She said, "You children act like we done won a lottery or something." I grabbed Mom by the arms and before she knew it I had spun her around, she said, "Jessie, if you don't let me go, I may change my mind."

I knew she was kidding, but I didn't want to take any chances. I dipped her first, though, and ran out of the room laughing. Carmen was still jumping up and down, saying over and over again, "Spin me, Jessie. Spin me like you did Mom." I patted her on top of her head, and went into my room to think and revel in my victory. I laid across my bed and stared at the ceiling. Things were really beginning to get better for my family. I couldn't wait until tomorrow, I could almost see the expression on Patrick's face. I started pinching myself to make sure I wasn't dreaming. Thank God, I wasn't. Mom was finally coming around, and I was one step closer to my heavenly father.

When I woke up the next morning, I quickly took my shower, and dressed for school. Willie and Aaron were both talking about how sleepy they were. I told them I didn't care, because they knew that today was a school day, so they should have gotten in bed earlier. Willie came out of our bedroom rubbing his eyes. Aaron had made it to the bathroom and was sitting on the toilet nodding back off. I couldn't help but to laugh, because this was a routine for them, to wake up dragging on Monday mornings. I had told them to go to sleep and to quit playing last night. I knew that this was going to happen. They could be so silly and always were up to something goofy. As soon as I turned the lights off, I felt someone tickling my toes. I snatched by feet back. All of a sudden they burst out laughing—this wasn't good enough, though, they decided that they wanted to start snatching covers. I couldn't take any more of their clowning around, so I got up and tackled both of them. I know I knocked the breath out of them, Aaron, with his twisted sense of humor, laughed and said, "The boy's sleepwalking; he thinks he playing football."

I told them if they didn't leave me alone and go to sleep, I was going to get Mom, and they knew what was going to happen if I disturbed her when she's sleeping, especially this time of night. I'm surprised the noise from me tackling them didn't wake her up, I guess she and Carmen were exhausted from all the excitement that had gone on today. Aaron got smart and said, "Jessie, you make me sick. Can't nobody even have any fun around you."

I said, "I'm not thinking about what either one of you squirts thinks, now go to sleep." The room was quiet for a few minutes, then I heard Willie whispering to Aaron about how they would see who could stay up the longest, "but let's wait until our boring roommate goes to sleep." That's the last I remember. I guess that's what they did.

I couldn't wait to get to school. All I could think about was seeing Patrick and giving the good news, I knew that he was going to be just as happy for me as I was about Mom letting me go to church—at least it's a start for me. Willie and Aaron were finally dressed, and arguing in the kitchen about who was going to get the prize out of the cereal box. The fussing woke Mom, and she walked in the kitchen and I knew by the look on her face that she was angry, because they had interrupted her sleep. She snatched the prize out of Aaron's hand and said, "I get the prize. Now you two, hurry up and eat, before you're late for school."

Aaron said, "Yes, ma'am, but Willie got the prize last time." Mom said, "I don't care who got it last time, I'm sick of you two fussing all the time about something. If you've got to fuss about toys all the time, I'll just have to start taking them; and I'll have to tell Patrick's mother to stop sending them to you, because y'all can't play fair with each other."

They both started talking at the same time. Willie began his plea-bargain, "Please, Mom," he said, "we'll start acting better, and we'll try not to argue so much."

Aaron started his line of defense. "That's right, Mom, we're sorry. I promise we'll stop."

Mom just looked at them, because she knew that arguing was like breathing to them.

I asked Mom how she was feeling. "I'm all right, Jessie," she said. "I'm just angry at your knucklehead brothers. I hadn't planned on waking up this early. Next time I have to get up when I don't have to, I'm going to greet someone with a belt."

I looked at the clock—it was time for us to leave for school. I told Mom to lock the doors and for her and Carmen to be careful if they had to leave the house for anything. She said, "Okay, son, you know that I'm having the locks changed today, so you'll be getting a new set of keys."

"Good, Mom," I said, "I think all of us will sleep a lot better."

Then Mom said, "I had something to tell you, but I can't remember what it was—oh, I know, Jessie. Be sure to tell Mr. Moore that I'll be ready when he gets here tonight for my counseling session."

"I will, Mom. I know Mr. Moore will be glad to hear that."

We all said goodbye to Mom and I told her to give Carmen a kiss for me when she woke up. We raced to school. Of course I won because I was excited about the good news to deliver to my buddy Patrick, and I couldn't get there fast enough. When I got to school, Patrick was in the hall talking to one of our classmates. I spoke to them and headed toward my locker. Patrick quickly came over and said, "How's it going?"

"Great," I said, "just great. I've got something to tell you. I know it will be music to your ears. Right now we don't have time to really talk, I wish we did, but we can talk during lunch."

Patrick said, "Give me a hint, Jessie,"

"Church," I said.

Patrick started grinning, then he said, "I think I already know, as a matter of fact, I'm sure I know, plus by the look on your face, Jessie, I know it's not bad news."

"You got that right," I said as the second bell rang.

Patrick said, "See you later, Jessie, I've gotta go before I'm late for class."

I quickly got my books out of the locker and rushed to my class because I didn't want to be late. I could hardly sit still in class. I kept watching the clock, I was able to concentrate better on my school work, though, and it felt good not having so many problems on my mind. I soon found my mind drifting off on Mom. I wondered what she and Carmen were doing. I hoped that Randle wouldn't show up at the house today, that's all Mom needed was to have him threatening her again, especially now, when she's made her mind up to get help. Oh, yeah, I almost forgot, I needed to give Mr. Moore the message for Mom.

The rustling of books and paper interrupted my thoughts—lunchtime had approached. I rushed out of class toward my locker. I had to put my books up, and I needed to catch Mr. Moore before he reached the cafeteria. When I got to his office he was talking to a student. I knew it would probably be a while before his conference was over, and I didn't want to be late meeting Patrick for lunch. I'll come back later, I thought.

I met Patrick outside where we usually ate lunch. When I got there he asked me where I had been, because he could hardly wait to talk to me and that his ears couldn't hold out any longer. I told him that I had to stop by Mr. Moore's office.

"For what?" he asked. I couldn't answer him right away; I really didn't know what to say or how to begin. I hadn't told him about Mom's drinking problem. I guess I had been too ashamed, and didn't know how he would feel about me. Even though he was my best friend, I felt that I had to keep Mom's drinking problem a secret, but I didn't know why I was ashamed or what I was really ashamed of—was it my mother getting drunk, or was it my own selfish pride? I knew I had to pray about this, because I didn't want to ever feel embarrassed about telling the truth again, yet I felt a need to protect my mother's character.

"I just needed to give him a message, Patrick. It's not important, but what I have to tell you is." I ripped open a bag of chips while I was talking. Patrick was eating a sandwich. "Patrick, I got a chance to ask Mom whether I could start going to church with you, and whether it was okay with her if I got baptized. She said I could."

Patrick smiled and said, "That's great, Jessie."

Then I told Patrick that Mom said she needed time to think about me getting baptized, but she made feel better when she said that she and my sister and brothers would be at church if she said yes. "Patrick, man, I am so happy. I can't remember when Mom has ever gone to church, yet she said she would come to see me get baptized."

Patrick smiled and said, "That's the best news I've heard all day, but Jessie, there is something I want to ask you. I don't mean to seem like I'm butting into your business, but I can't understand why your mother couldn't go ahead and give you permission to get baptized if she said you could come to church. How come she has to think about you getting baptized?"

I replied, "I don't know, Patrick, I've asked myself the same questions. I think it may be because Mom has had so much on her mind, and I know that she has been under a lot of pressure lately. She told me yesterday that her mind was full, and she couldn't think clear. But look at it like this, Patrick; she could have said no to church and no to me being baptized, but she didn't. That's why I know that I'll be getting baptized real soon, and my family will be there with me. She gave me her promise on that."

Then Patrick said, "Jessie, I remember when I got baptized—I think I was eleven or twelve years old—I walked around the church bragging to my friends about how I was ready to be baptized. These were some the same friends who saw me dive off of a diving board and do a belly whopper at a pool party one Saturday. To top that off, I knew I couldn't swim—I was just trying to show off. Everybody was flipping off of the diving board, doing all kinds of stunts. Not to be out-done, I decided to do a fancy flip and almost drowned. I was pulled out of the water by the boy's dad who lived at the house—talk about kicking and fighting! I was in four-foot water. I just knew it was over for me, kaput, I was a goner, trying to make a showing for a girl."

"What girl, Patrick?" I asked.

"Melinda," he said.

"Four-eyed Melinda with the buckteeth?" I jokingly asked.

"I don't know what you're talking about, Jessie," Patrick jokingly said, "she looked good to me, and her teeth ain't bucked."

"Whatever you say, Patrick," I laughed and said, "but when you get through talking, that girl can't close her mouth for them big teeth poking out. Well, what happened when they pulled you out of the water, Patrick?" I asked.

Patrick, still taking a bite out of his sandwich, said, "Jessie, I was shocked. It amazed me how quickly they forgot they were worried about me when they thought my life was in danger. After they got me out of the water and saw that I was all right, that's when the joking started—everybody was laughing, even my so-called friends, talking about all I had to do was stand up. They said the water was only four feet and I was about 5 feet, 7 inches tall. They started calling me 'the belly whopper teenybopper.' They even made up a song about me. I couldn't believe those creeps, they were walking around me in circles, singing, 'the belly whopper teenybopper decided to take a swim. Splish splash bam, splish splash bam. Look out for that body slam, belly whopper teenybopper, don't get into the water again, unless you remember to put on a pair of safety fins.' I was so embarrassed I made my mind up then that I wasn't ever going to risk my life again trying to show off for a stuck-up girl. Now when these same so-called friends at church heard that I was getting baptized, they couldn't wait to remind me of that pool party, which they said they would have named the 'big splash,' had they known I was going to put on a show. But to make a long story short, on the day I got baptized, all of them showed up for church. Some of them hadn't been there since last Easter, and won't be back probably until Christmas. They sat there, according to Mom, like they were watching a movie, Momma said, some of them sitting next to her had enough nerves to whisper that they hoped brother Miller snatched Patrick up quick, because if he don't, Patrick gonna start fighting the water. I didn't, though, the baptism was a wonderful experience for me. I was a little afraid at first, because I started having flashbacks of the diving-board incident, then brother Miller whispered in my ear that everything was going to be all right. I was fine after that. Jessie, you wouldn't believe the audience I had that Sunday. Momma told me that it was divine intervention, because some of them could have been on the streets, getting into trouble, but instead they were in church."

I told Patrick not to feel bad, that I couldn't swim either, but after that fish story, I thought that I was going to learn, not because I was afraid of getting baptized, but because I might need him to pull me out of my bathtub one day and would never hear the end of how he had to rescue his buddy.

"Okay, Jessie," Patrick replied, "you're trying to pay me back. I see you're not going to let me forget the fact that I teased you about your nose getting stuck in your bathtub drain."

"That's right, Patrick, you know I have a memory like an elephant."

Patrick couldn't resist the opportunity for one of his wise cracks. Abruptly, he said, "and a nose like one, too. You're prepared to travel wherever you go."

At that moment the school bell rang for 4th-period class. "Patrick, you lucked out this time," I said, "be thankful that you were saved by the bell. Otherwise you just missed out on my imitation of Mike Tyson."

Patrick immediately flexed that little skinny arm, appearing to search for a muscle. He looked at me and said, "Boy, you don't want me to start preaching. Rev. Slick gonna lay hands on you. Rev Slick gonna whip some Holy Ghost in that boy."

I kept walking—friend or no friend, Patrick's jokes were corny at times. I had to meet with Mr. Moore before school was out. I made sure I went back to Mr. Moore's office to let him know that Momma would be waiting for him to pick her up for her meeting. Mr. Moore said that he was happy to see Momma willing to go, because he had experienced in the past, some alcoholics, such as a good friend of his, who promised to attend group therapy, then decided at the last minute that they didn't need anyone telling them how to stop drinking. Rather than deal with others with the same problems or addictions, they tried to stop themselves. Unfortunately, they ended up worse off than before—either hospitalized or locked up behind bars for drunk driving. He asked me how the family was doing. I told him that we were doing a lot better since Momma had not been drinking. I also told him that Momma had gotten upset and had come close to drinking again.

Mr. Moore looked worried, then asked, "Does your mother have any alcohol around the house, Jessie?"

I told him that I didn't think so, and that I hadn't seen any, but it really concerned me when she told me she wanted a drink because she had gotten so upset. Mr. Moore asked me what had caused Momma to feel this way. I hesitantly replied, "It's a long story. Momma finally realizes that Randle, who also drinks, is a no-good deadbeat, and she's really afraid of him. He has a violent temper and he fights her all the time. Mom's even told him that she didn't want to see him anymore, but he came over to our house a few days ago and tried to force his way in. I know that this is what caused Momma to want a drink. Mr. Moore, please don't tell Momma that I talked to you about this, because I don't know whether she even wanted me to mention any of this to you."

Mr. Moore looked at me and said, "Jessie, whenever you and I speak, everything is said in confidence. What's said behind my door and in my office, stays in here, son. I know the importance of having someone you can trust enough to confide in and not have your confidence betrayed. Why do you think I've been in this profession so long? Let me say this, if every time a student, parent or teacher enters my office with a personal problem and I blabbed it all over the place, I never would have anyone coming in here. Do you understand or feel a little bit better now?"

"Yes, sir, I understand and I didn't mean any harm. I just didn't want Momma finding out that I had discussed her business. I know one thing, I'm glad that she is not seeing Randle anymore, because that man is crazy and my Momma is just too good to be with him. She's better off without him. I'm just glad she realized it before it was too late."

Mr. Moore smiled and asked me how classes were going for Willie and Aaron. "Things are going fine, Mr. Moore," I said, "it was a little hard to get them to do their homework the other day, only because they wanted to go out and play, but I made them do it anyway. I'm even able to concentrate a lot better on my school work now. Mr. Moore, I was hoping that Momma told you about what was really causing us to miss school and why our grades were dropping. I lied to you and said that everything at home was all right, only because I was afraid to tell you about her being an alcoholic. I didn't know what you would do."

Mr. Moore reached over and patted me on the shoulder, his big hand almost knocking me to the floor. "I understand, Jessie," he said. "The important thing is that the problem is now out in the open, and your mother gets treatment for her alcoholism; therefore, your mind and your sister's and brothers' minds will not be clouded by the emotional turmoil and fear that manifests itself in the families of an alcoholic. That's why the family counseling was suggested. But, first of all, your mother has to get over one hurdle before she goes over another one. She's almost like a baby who's beginning to walk again, and she needs her loved ones to support her, to keep her from falling flat on her face when she begins to lift herself up and walk upright. Jessie, I want you to be her driving force when you see her not wanting to take those steps. Right now she's in the crawling stage, but she's not alone. Tonight she'll get a chance to see and hear other alcoholics who want to reform themselves. Hopefully she'll open up and speak out about what the drinking was doing to her and how it was affecting her relationship—not only with you all, but her relationship with her own level of self-esteem. Sometimes a new member only observes the others their first night or so, but once they see that they are all in the same boat, so to speak, they soon open up and speak freely about their own personal drinking problem."

I thought to myself, Mr. Moore really is going out of his way to help us. Then I blurted out, "Mr. Moore, I really appreciate you for helping our Momma, and I know she does, too. If there's ever anything that I can do for you, please let me know." I laughed and said, "Even if it's taking out the garbage."

Mr. Moore smiled and replied, "Well, Jessie, on that note, we'll end our conversation, and what you said about taking out the garbage I'm going to hold you to that one, so don't get a sudden case of amnesia, when you come to visit me and look like you don't know what I'm talking about. Speaking of garbage, tonight your Momma, in a sense, will be working on getting rid of what she would call a form of garbage in her life."

At first I didn't know what Mr. Moore meant, then I realized that he was talking about the alcohol. I told Mr. Moore that I would see him later and left. I always found myself leaving his office feeling confident and a lot better, and whether Mr. Moore realized this or not, he was really making a difference in my family's life. I often wondered why he had never married, because he was always lending a helping hand to others. I had heard other students say the same thing about him! He was definitely not a phony. I remember him saying once that he sometimes felt that he was married to his job, and all the kids at school were like his children. I was thinking he was married, because I would see a woman with two small children visit him at the school. I found out later that the woman was his sister, and the children were Mr. Moore's nephew and niece. I thought they were his children because he had pictures of them on his desk in his office. Now I know why Momma would sometimes say, "What may look like a certain situation to us may be totally different from what the situation really is."

I had a few more minutes left before my study hall was over, so I decided to write Momma a poem. How do I begin it? There was so much I wanted to say. Oh God, I thought, please let me write something that will inspire or encourage her. Soon the words begin to slowly flow across the paper...

(MOTHER'S EYES)

I looked into my mother's eyes and found myself within

I put my hand within her hand, and felt my life begin

I touched her heart and felt it beat, my heart no longer stood still

I felt the air slowly enter my lungs, then I began to live

She may have thought I can't give love, but she did

She may have thought I do love you, yes she did

But whatever her reason, whatever her thoughts, she's my mother

I wouldn't have it any other way, because I truly truly love her

I looked into my mother's eyes and found myself within

I raised my hand and touched her face, and felt her love transcend

I looked into my mother's eyes and knew the love she felt

I touched the tears that moistened her cheek, and saw the joy that dwelt

She may have said I don't care, but she does

LeNora Millen

She may have said I love you. Indeed she does

But whatever her reason, whatever her thoughts, she's my mother

I wouldn't have it any other way, because I truly truly love her

Within her eyes, within her face, I know within her heart

It beats with love, it beats with joy, it beats the sound of hope

The love of a mother and the love of a child, is such a beautiful sight

That's why when I looked into my mother's eyes I found life

CHAPTER 5

I met Patrick when school was over; Aaron and Willie were already at the front of the school building. Willie was excited about winning the spelling bee in his class, and he didn't waste any time boring us all the way home with his list of words he wanted us to spell. Patrick pulled a fast one on him though, he said, "Willie, I got a word I bet you can't spell."

Willie stuck his chest out and said, "I bet I can, Patrick. What's the word? I know I can spell it."

Patrick looked at me and winked, then said, "Spell 'shut up'! I know you can't spell that, now, can you?"

Aaron couldn't help but to join in, and said, "Yeah, smarty pants, spell it and do it, too."

Willie looked at Patrick—if looks could kill. He rolled his eyes so hard at him that I thought they were going to get stuck. We couldn't help but laugh. Poor Willie didn't say another word until we got home, Patrick said he would see me at school tomorrow and headed home. He didn't have far to go since he lived two streets away from me.

All of a sudden Willie yelled out, "I bet y'all chumps can't spell idiots." I guess he had to let a little steam off; he wasn't one to be outdone, not Willie, he just had to have the last word. Aaron and I just ignored him and walked up the steps to the house. Upon entering the house Carmen met me.

Carmen met me with her hand stuck out. She knew I usually stopped by Mr. Charlie's store on the way home from school. Of course I had a lollipop for her. She gave me a big grin; she really looked funny since she had lost her two upper front teeth.

"Where's Momma, Carmen?" I asked.

"She's in her room ironing her clothes, Jessie," Carmen said. "We have to go over to Mama Rose's house, since she has to go to her meeting." Carmen started to get impatient and asked, "Jessie, can we go now?"

"No," I said. "Momma already told me that her meeting isn't until 6 o'clock tonight, so we don't have to go to Mama Rose's house until 5:30."

Carmen started pouting because she knew she would have to wait. I went in Mom's room and told her that Mr. Moore said he'd be here on time to take her to the meeting.

She said, "Good, Jessie. I really appreciate his help. You don't think I'm causing him any inconvenience, do you?"

I said, "Naw, Momma, he told me today how happy he was about you deciding to get therapy; we all are, Momma; you're not an inconvenience to any of us."

Momma smiled and her eyes twinkled somewhat. I reached into my pocket and pulled out the poem that I had written for her. As I unfolded the paper, I said, "Momma, we love you so much no matter what, and I can't say it enough. I had some extra time left at school today. My mind was on you and I felt a need to write something special for you, that's why I wrote this poem. I hope you like it."

As I handed the paper to Momma, she looked somewhat puzzled, then she sat on the edge of her bed and read my poem. Silence filled the room; it was so quiet at that moment that the slow drip from the bathroom faucet seemed to grow louder and faster. I studied Mom's face as she was reading; her hands were trembling as she held the paper, then a smile came across her face. She looked at me with watery eyes and said, "Jessie, this is a beautiful poem, son. Did you really write it? It sounds like something out of one of those poetry books I used to read in school."

I said, "Yes, ma'am; it's your poem from me."

Momma smiled and said, "Jessie, I didn't know you could write poetry."

"I didn't, either, Momma, but the words came so easy and they came from my heart. I meant every word."

Momma started crying. I sat on the bed next to her and held her hand. I told her that I didn't mean to make her cry with the poem. I just wanted her to be happy. She wiped her eyes with a towel she had grabbed out of the clothes basket next to the bed, and said "Jessie, I'm not sad. These are tears of joy. I can remember being upset and telling you and the other children how I wished I'd never gave birth to any of you. I was angry with myself, and with the direction my life was headed. I have to admit that I dealt with my anger and frustration the wrong way. I took my anger out on you all, even when the relationships with some of the so-called men in my life went bad, I blamed you and the other children. Yet my children never abandoned me, I abandoned you all emotionally and physically and became my own children's worst nightmare. If any of you ever got angry at me you had a right to, because I was not acting like a mother."

I didn't want Momma to get herself too upset to attend her meeting by feeling guilty, so I told her to stop crying and stop blaming herself, because we were only concerned with her getting help. To relieve the tension, I asked for one of Mom's bear hugs. She smiled and hugged me as tightly as she could. Jokingly I said, "Mom, you can do better than that." I told Momma to go wash her face because all of her makeup was smearing up. She laughed and headed toward the bathroom. I went into the kitchen to get her a glass of water.

When I walked back into Mom's room with the water, she had picked my poem up off of the bed and was reading it again. I stood at the door because I didn't want to interrupt her. After she finished reading it she placed the poem up against her chest and hugged it as if it were a person; then I heard her whisper and say, "I love you, too, son. I love all of you."

Momma got dressed early that evening, and we ate dinner earlier than usual. She told all of us to behave while at Mama Rose's and to stay indoors. I told her that we had to do our homework anyway, so that should keep us busy for a while.

A horn was soon heard blowing outside. Willie ran to the window and yelled out, "It's Mr. Moore, Momma, he's getting out of the car."

Momma said "Well, open the door, then, while I get my purse." Mr. Moore was greeted with smiles as he walked in. It seemed strange having him stand in the living room, since we usually saw him at school. Willie and Aaron could be heard whispering about Mr. Moore's shiny shoes. I talked over them and told him that Momma would be out in a few minutes. "She just went into the room to get her purse," I said.

Mr. Moore clapped his hands together and said, "That's all right, son, I'm early, anyway." Within minutes, Momma stepped into the living room. She looked at Mr. Moore and spoke. He smiled and asked her how she was doing.

"I guess I'll do, Mr. Moore," she said.

Mr. Moore smiled and said, "Let's get rid of the formality—feel free to call me 'Mitchell.'" Momma blushed and said, "All right, Mitchell." Then she said, "Well, in that case, you can call me Betty."

Those two were really warming up to each other. Mr. Moore must have picked up on Mom's nervousness. He seemed to calm her fears by explaining to her that everyone was nervous their first night, but that she'd soon feel at ease.

Momma smiled and said, "If I run out tonight, I hope you're fast enough to catch me."

Mr. Moore looked shocked. Momma smiled and said, "I'm just rambling off out of nervousness—don't pay me any attention." It was time for Momma to leave, so we stood watching Mom get in Mr. Moore's car. We waved goodbye and walked down the street to Mama Rose's house. When we arrived at Mama Rose's she was standing in the door waiting on us. Carmen started running up the steps and grabbed open the screen door; it's funny how she thought she was the boss whenever we went down there. Mama Rose was really nice, she had told us a few years ago to call her "Mama Rose" and we've been calling her that ever since. As soon as Carmen got in the door she got her usual hug and kiss. Mama Rose looked at me and said, "You know, I'm mad at you, Jessie. You promised me that you were going to fix that broke leg on my favorite chair, and you never did show up. Too bad, son, because I fixed your favorite dessert, banana pudding, but I had to eat it up all by myself."

I smiled and said, "I'll fix it, Mama Rose. You know I don't mind doing anything for you—something just came up."

She looked at me and said, "Come here, boy, you're not to big to hug." Then she planted one of those wet kisses on my jaw. I could hear Aaron and Willie snickering. they knew how I felt about Mama Rose leaving her wet kisses on my face. Mama Rose was squeezing me so hard that I thought that she was going to smother me with that big chest of hers. She finally let me go, thank God, I said to myself, now it was Willie and Aaron's turn to get their face wet. Carmen jealously stood by. She couldn't stand all the attention Mama Rose was giving us—as far as Carmen was concerned, she was Mama Rose's little muffin, and we were taking away her privileges when we came around.

I still laugh when I think about how Carmen got the name "little muffin." One Saturday Mama Rose baked us some blueberry muffins, Carmen's favorite. They smelled so good that Carmen couldn't sit still. Mama Rose took them out of the oven and told us that as soon as they cooled off, we could eat them. Carmen mysteriously disappeared and we later found her and the muffins on Mama Rose's back porch—out of a dozen muffins, there were only four left. Carmen went home with a stomachache and a new name, Little Muffin. Mama Rose was so tickled, she couldn't get angry. Of course we were angry, because the three of us had only one muffin. Mama

Rose took the fourth one out of Carmen's hand and ate it. Mama Rose baked a chocolate cake earlier that day, and said that we could get a slice after we ate dinner before Carmen got to it, too. Aaron told her that we had already eaten dinner early because Momma had to go to her meeting. I know his mouth was watering for that chocolate cake. I told Aaron that we needed to get our homework first. He frowned and told Willie that I was trying to be grown, by telling them what to do.

Mama Rose quickly responded, "No homework, no food or cake." I don't think I'd ever seen Aaron get into his schoolbooks so fast. Once our homework was done, Mama Rose had our cake already cut and our milk poured into the glasses. She was even nice enough to wrap some food and cake for us to take home. After we ate, I went ahead and fixed the chair. It wasn't hard to repair, since the nails had only worn away from the wood. It made me feel good to be able to do something for Mama Rose, since she always found a way to help us, even feed us. If Momma needed something she would send what she had. Even if it was only a package of beans, they filled our stomach.

Aaron and I carried the chair into the living room and told Mama Rose that her favorite chair was ready for her to sit in. "Thank you, baby," she said in a that high-pitched voice of hers that always reminded me of those sweet old ladies they show on television. She leaned over and put her cushion in the chair and said, "I don't think my back was going to hold out any longer in that little hard chair I had been sitting in lately."

"Go ahead Mama Rose, try it out," I said. She sat in her chair and smiled, as a matter of fact she stayed in that chair, even nodding at times, until we left. Momma let Carmen spend the night since she was asleep. We knew by the expression on Mama's Rose's face that she didn't really want to wake her Little Muffin.

I could hardly wait to hear about Mom's meeting. Mama Rose asked her how everything had gone on her first night, and surprisingly enough Momma said that she had really enjoyed it. Momma gave Mama Rose a hug, as usual, and told her that she would be back the next morning for Carmen. Mama Rose seemed distracted, but soon gave herself away after repeatedly looking over Mom's shoulder as if she was looking for someone. She abruptly asked Mom where Mr. Moore was.

Mom, sort of blushing said, "Well, Mama Rose, you know I didn't want to hold Mitchell up any longer, he seemed sort of tired and I felt like walking even though he seemed to think it was not a good idea. I twisted his arm and had him drop me off, of course in front of the house."

I could see that Mama Rose's curiosity was peaking. She looked at Mom, winked and said, "Betty, that Mr. Mitchell sho' is a fine specimen of a man. Is he single, girl?"

Mom couldn't help but laugh, then said, "As far as I know, Mama Rose. Why are you asking? You want a date with him?"

Mama Rose replied in a chuckle, "Baby, don't count Mama Rose out. If you don't snatch that tall, good-looking man, Mama Rose gonna spray the WD40 on the joints and pounce him."

Mom started laughing so hard that she was in tears. I was sort of shocked at Mama Rose's comment, talking about pouncing Mr. Moore, gonna give herself a heart attack. Get two giggling women together and this is what happens. I stood listening, as intently as not to be noticed, before Mom gave an answer to the question Mama Rose had asked about Mr. Moore. My presence seemed uninvited and I was quickly sent out of the room. This was a habit of theirs—send the children out of the room when grown folks want to discuss something they think we shouldn't hear. If only they knew the truth about what some of our young generation really knew.

I could probably give them a few pointers on how a gentleman was to treat a young lady. I strained my ears to hear Mom's answer, yet all I could hear was whispering. I was able to hear Mom saying, "Mama Rose, only time will tell. You know I've got to get my act together before I even think about dating."

Once we got outside, the night air felt wonderful as we walked home. There was so much excitement in the air, all of us were talking at the same time. We wanted Momma to tell us about her meeting, Mom smiled and said, "Wait till we get home."

As we neared the stairs to the house, Momma suddenly stopped. I noticed she was looking up toward the sky. The sky was so clear that night; the stars were twinkling as if they were dancing amongst themselves. Willie and Aaron, seeing Mom stop dead in her tracks to only stare at the sky, could be heard asking, "Mom, what are you looking at? Why don't you answer us, Mom?"

Mom seemed distracted, almost as if she were in a trance, still not answering them. I walked over to Mom and asked her whether she was all right; she was still looking up toward the sky. Mom only stared into the twilight of the beautiful stars, and in almost a whisper said, "I saw a falling star, Jessie. I haven't seen a falling star since I was about ten years old. I was making a wish, son."

I didn't ask her what she wished for, but I think I know. Once Willie and Aaron heard that Momma had seen a falling star, they wanted to stay outside to see whether they could see another one. I told them that it wouldn't be likely; we could be out there all night looking for another one. Once we got in the house and changed into our pajamas, Momma started telling us about her meeting. She said Mr. Moore really gave her courage by being there with her—because she knew that she would not have been able to go that route without him.

Aaron looked at Mom and said, "Momma, tell us how everything went. What did you say? Were you scared? How many people were there?"

Momma said, "Slow down, Aaron, you don't give me a chance to answer one question before you're asking me another one." Momma sat back in the chair and said, "Let me see where I'm going to start. Well, first of all, I want to say this about what I heard. I realized tonight that people from all walks of life can be and are affected by alcoholism. I was told tonight that I was just another statistic. When I entered the room I began to freeze up. Mitchell realized this and whispered in my ear for me to hang on in there. We all sat in our chairs, which were in a circular shape. The other new members and I were introduced to the group. Everyone was really open about their drinking problems; we were told that this type of group therapy could help to build a closer bond with one another, as well as with our families. No one there was to look at the other alcoholic as if they were in worse condition than they were, because an alcoholic is an alcoholic. Our group consisted of counselors who had united to assist other alcoholics back to abstinence."

 I asked Momma why they used rehabilitated alcoholics to counsel the alcoholics needing help. I couldn't see how they could help anyone. Momma took a deep breath and said, "Jessie, ironically enough one of the ladies in tonight's meeting had asked almost the same question." She said that she didn't feel that their guidance was reliable. "Strangely enough," she said, "we were told that until you walk down the same road that a person has traveled or experience the same problems that the person has tackled, then your position is that of an outsider looking in. The person who's dealt firsthand with the same addiction, illness, isolation—what have you—only this person can truly relate to or identify with the person who needs help.

Only this person," Mom explained, "can tap into the feelings and needs of their addictions. This is why our therapy session is so unique; it consists of counselors who have dealt with the disease of alcoholism. They are the positive force behind getting our lives back in order, the counselors had been there and back. They have struggled with their alcoholism and decided to take charge of their lives. Self-control and a strong will and desire to solve his or her personal drinking problem was their mission. That is why these counselors are able to gain the trust and respect of alcoholics such as myself and others who were there tonight. In a sense we all have a story to tell about how our addictions have come close to destroying not only ourselves, but also those close to our hearts. Our families suffer with this disease, as well, son. And as I said earlier, the alcoholic can come from all walks of life, and from any profession. Two of our members tonight were attorneys; I met a schoolteacher who spoke about drinking between classes. I met a dentist who used mouthwash to conceal his alcoholic breath, until he drank so heavily on his lunch that he was found in a drunken stupor in the men's room. This, he said, cost him not only his license, but also the respect of his colleagues."

Willie listened intently, then asked, "Momma, did you say anything tonight?"

Mom reached over and rubbed the top of his head as she spoke. "As a matter of fact, Willie, your mother was able to tell the group a little about herself. It wasn't easy, but after I introduced myself, I slowly opened up when my time came to talk. I didn't think I could do it at first, and had made my mind up not to say anything, but before I knew it, I was talking about my drinking problem, how it started, and how it was turning me into a monster. I think what touched them more was when I discussed how Jessie had helped me to see that I needed to get help. I explained to them about how you and my other children suffered by trying to protect me. I started crying while I spoke, but it felt good, because I realized that me needing therapy was nothing to be ashamed of. I knew then that I was part of a problem in that room that affected all of us—maybe in different ways, but the disease was the same. As I looked around the room I could see that these people that I had never met in my entire life, with the exception of Mitchell, were all hurting. And that before the night was over, we would hurt for each other. One woman sitting next to me broke down crying while she discussed what had happened in her life. Before I knew it, I was crying because I could relate to her suffering. I didn't think I had any more tears left after I had poured my heart out earlier that night. I remember grabbing her hand and holding it until we left the meeting. It was obvious that this woman was in a great deal of pain. It's really unbelievable how some of us bonded almost instantly with each other. I remember one of the counselors telling her to let it out—the anger, the hurt, whatever it was. She was really beaten up emotionally; she was hanging on by a thread, I suppose. As hard as it was for her, she finally was able to talk. She said that, because of her drinking problem, she had lost her seven-year-old son in a custody battle with her husband. She said she didn't blame her husband, because he had tried to work things out with her by not pulling the courts into their fights. The final straw was when she got filthy drunk and didn't remember to pick their son up from school. She said the school ended up contacting her ex-husband after their attempts were unsuccessful in reaching her. He came to her home, looked through the window, and saw her on the floor. He thought that, maybe, something was seriously wrong with her. He ended up kicking in the front door. She said her ex-husband found her sprawled out on the living-room floor drunk, still holding her bottle of gin. Her son, already being upset because of the door having to be kicked in, started screaming at her, saying over and over again that she didn't love him, she only loved her whiskey, and ran out of the house in tears. She said that, although her ex-husband told their son that she was getting help for her drinking problem, she said that her son doesn't want to talk to her. She wept and said that her own flesh and blood was afraid that she would start drinking and yelling at him again. Her son, she said, has told his father that he was afraid that his mother was turning into a monster and might hurt him. Even though she told her ex-husband that she understood, she said it hurt like hell having your own son too afraid to talk to his mother even on the telephone. She said that she was determined that she was going to get help, and that no alcohol in this world was worth not being with her son."

Momma also told us about a man in her group who described himself as being a heavy drinker since the age of fifteen. She said he was a stockbroker and when the stock market crashed, he felt his world had also crashed around him. He said he thought his only way out was to drink, because, while he was sober, he was too in-touch with himself, yet by being drunk he could somehow drink his problems away. Momma said hearing his admission frightened her, because she didn't realize the serious nature of withdrawal symptoms. Momma told us about how the man said that his withdrawals from the alcohol were life-threatening to him and he had to be placed in the hospital, because he had developed seizures as a result of the withdrawals.

Willie looked worried as Momma spoke. Then he asked her what she meant by "withdrawals," and he wanted to know whether Momma had experienced any of whatever they were. Momma said that the way the counselors explained the withdrawals, which is common with any type of addiction, was trembling, sweating, and insomnia, along with other symptoms which could vary on an individual basis. She said that people also hallucinate sometimes as quickly as a day or two after they stop drinking and there are other symptoms of withdrawal that they mentioned that she couldn't remember.

Mom was quite honest with us. She didn't want to mislead us or pretend to have accomplished a great miracle in beating this disease. She explained to us that she would have to read as much literature as possible to learn more about the effects of alcohol, and as she tackled this addiction, she wanted us to be patient with her.

During the course of the conversation, Momma told us something that really frightened me. She said that she had experienced some type of withdrawal, at times. She said, at first, she didn't know what was going on and that it wasn't a very pleasant feeling. She looked at us and said, "Y'all didn't know this, because I didn't want to frighten any of you. I had talked to Mitchell about them, even had to call him on more than one occasion when y'all were still in school. I was told by one of the counselors tonight that I was fortunate enough to be there now, because the longer the alcoholic goes without treatment, the more severe the disease and withdrawals. He also explained to us that any alcoholic will have some type of relapse after putting the bottle down—or should I say, after they stop drinking. I found out that the reason I had been depressed was because of this."

Aaron seemed almost hesitant to ask questions, for whatever reason, tonight, but said, "Momma, I'm glad you went on and got help. I didn't know that after you stopped drinking all of that other stuff could happen to you. I thought all you had to do was leave the alcohol alone."

Momma smiled and said, "Aaron, I wish it were that easy, but, sad to say, it's not. There is a price to pay and the reward is not worth the gain."

Aaron asked Momma whether she was what they called the "heavy drinker."

Momma said, "I can say I am. It really didn't take much to get me drunk, Aaron, and it really didn't matter, because I would be just as dangerous behind the wheel of a car, or just as violent as the long-term heavy drinker. The disease is the same, only the withdrawal symptoms that the other alcoholics and me had were different. Let me say this to you, boys, because I worry about how my drinking has affected my children. I wouldn't wish this addiction of mine on any of you. Your lives are too important to waste your minds on alcohol, drugs—any of that junk. What's a quick high compared to a clear mind and a high level of self-esteem? You can go far with that, but how far can you go high on drugs or intoxicated beyond reasoning? Nowhere but to an early grave. I want you boys to remember this: your Momma may not have been a good example to you in the last few months or so, but it's never too late to get back on track."

My mind took me back to the day Momma got extremely upset when Randle came over. I remembered how nervous she was—she even wanted a drink that day. She came close to drinking. Thank God she hadn't.

Momma told us about other admissions that had been made in her group therapy. She said it was really an emotional session. Before they let out, Momma said that they were told by the counselors that they would have frequent group meetings where they could talk about their past and present troubles, and that everyone there was each other's support, along with the support of their families.

Momma said they gave them the most important admission of an alcoholic—first of all, she said the alcoholic had to get through the denial stage and admit to being an alcoholic and how his or her life had been uprooted, torn apart, unmanageable and so forth. Momma read from a list of several other admissions. The admission that caught my ear was the serenity prayer. Mom knew that this prayer got my attention, because I got her to read it again.

Momma said she had a lot more to tell us, but she would have to tomorrow, because she was getting sleepy. She got up out of her chair, stretched and let out big yawn. While her mouth was still open, she said, "I'll see y'all in the morning. I'm pooped."

I found myself getting sleepy, too. I headed for the bed and pounced onto the mattress so hard that dust flew in the air. Normally I'd sneeze, but I was too exhausted.

CHAPTER 6

As the days and weeks went by, our lives were being transformed for the better. We were slowly adjusting to Mom's hectic schedule. She seemed to stay on-the-go lately—as soon as she got home from work, she had to attend her meetings for her drinking problem. Most of the time we would have to stay with Mama Rose.

Finally one evening we were informed by Momma that we would be going to the meeting with her—she called the meetings "family group therapy." Willie and Aaron didn't want to go at first, because they were afraid. For some unknown reason they thought that they would be blamed for Mom's drinking problem. I asked Willie what had made them feel this way, and he said he remembered Momma would sometimes say, "You children drove me to drink." I tried to explain to them that Momma was speaking only out of anger and she really didn't mean it. Of course they didn't believe me, so I thought it would be best to go to Momma and ask her if she could talk to them, because they were confused and afraid. She said she would. She wanted them to go with her without feeling afraid or feeling that they were to blame for her illness.

Later that week Mr. Moore picked us up and drove us to the where Mom's counseling sessions would be held. I remember feeling a little nervous as we walked toward the group of people who I could see at the other end of the hall! I looked down at Carmen and smiled. She really didn't understand what was going on—all she knew was that we were going with Momma somewhere.

As we entered the room, I could feel my legs getting weak and a feeling of nausea in the pit of my stomach. "Oh no," I thought to myself, "don't faint—just take a deep breath, Jessie, and stay calm." I kept saying this over and over in my mind until I felt better. Carmen must have picked up on my nervousness, because she wouldn't let go of my hand, and was like my shadow. Every step I took she would be on the heel of my shoe.

As we approached the chairs I noticed several people looking in our direction. I could hear an older woman comment, "Those have to Betty's children—that little girl is the spitting image of her."

I tried to sit Carmen in the chair next to me; instead she whispered in my ear asking whether she could sit in my lap. She looked so afraid, I guess the strange faces in the room frightened her. Willie and Aaron sat quietly during the meeting as the counselors spoke. Mom appeared proud of how well they paid attention to what was being discussed. As the evening dragged on Carmen began to nod and soon feel asleep. After about thirty minutes, Willie and Aaron could be heard snoring. I was too anxious to sleep. I wanted to remember as much as I could on this night, because I wanted to be able to help Momma as much as I could in her therapy. I knew that the only way I could support her was to understand, first of all, how to deal with her illness. I really learned a lot as I watched and listened to the counselors and others who sought help for their drinking problem. On occasion, I would feel Momma squeezing my hand, especially when one of the counselors spoke about how love in a family can be a positive turning point for the alcoholic, due to the bond in the family circle. He explained that this bond somehow strengthened the alcoholic, giving them a sense of hope, which indirectly could have a bearing on how they responded to treating their drinking problem.

As I listened to the counselors speak, I felt somewhat relieved in knowing that Momma was unconditionally loved by all of us, and we made sure that she knew it and heard it. We'd tell her we loved her on a day-today basis. This seemed to be her medicine of hope. I know she felt our love, because whenever we'd tell her how much we loved her, Mom's eyes would light up and she would soon flash that beautiful smile of hers—at times, even blushing as she often did.

I couldn't help but to look around the room at the other people who were attending family therapy. As I slowly searched their faces I could see that the illness of alcoholism was shared by all of us, in a sense, and this illness was not so much that of choice, but sometimes that of crying out for help. The cry for help echoed from all walks of life—rich and poor, with no particular nationality. The tears filling the eyes of those in pain had been shed by all of us at one point in our lives. I soon began to look differently at our situation at home. I made my mind up that night that I was going to deal with our problems as positively as I could, even though I still had many fears. I knew I had to deal with what was before me and before my family. I wasn't going to feel sorry for myself when things in life seemed unfair, even when life seemed to slap me directly in the face. I would not wallow in self-pity, because I could eventually drown myself in that sea of self-destructive pity. Instead I was able to muster up enough strength within my soul that I had never known existed. I felt almost like a baby chick who pecks away at the inside of its eggshell. Finally, by cracking the shell, it can glimpse light from the outside for the first time, yet the baby chick doesn't give up—the baby chick keeps pecking the shell until it finds its way out. I knew through it all there was light at the end of the tunnel for my family. I prayed silently to God and asked him to give me the knowledge and strength to be able to know the right things to do in life, in my decision-making.

My mind was so full, that night, I really took a lot in and felt good about our entire family being there.

As my eyes caught Mr. Moore's, he only smiled at me as if he were saying, "I'm proud of you, Jessie." He's given me this look before and it was always when I did something he approved of.

One of the counselors asked me a question that I thought I couldn't answer at first: "Jessie, your mother's illness has affected all of you in one way or another, and I know that it's been very difficult in dealing with her drinking problem. In your mind, Jessie, whose has been affected more by your mother's illness?" I thought to myself, "Why did he have to ask me this question? Out of all the people in this room he has to pick me out of the group with a tough question. How am I going to answer?" As I pondered over my answer my mind immediately focused on Momma—before I knew it, I was almost at the verge of blaming Momma for all of our problems. "I must be confused," I thought, "where are these emotions coming from?" I felt myself even getting angry with Mom for the way she just wandered off at times without an explanation as to her whereabouts. Thank God, I was able to remove the thought of self-pity and anger. My mind began to focus clearly as I evaluated my family's struggles. I began to feel ashamed of myself for wanting to put all the blame solely on Mom. "What about her feelings?" I thought. She was the one affected most; after all, she needed the cure for her illness. After a few minutes of soul-searching, I, in turn, answered the counselor by saying that, in my opinion, our mother, whom we all loved, had been affected more. I looked him directly in the eye and told him that because of my mother's drinking, she had given herself an illness that she had to cope with for the rest of her life. And whatever actions our Momma took toward us when she was drunk, I had to realize and remember that this person was not really my mother. I was dealing with a symptom of her illness, which caused her to act differently toward all of us.

As I spoke I could see the look on the counselor's face—it was a look of amazement. I guess my answer must have shocked him, yet he smiled as I spoke. I also told the counselor that, at first, I didn't look at our situation at home like I do now. "How did you feel about your younger brothers and sister, Jessie? What was going through your mind as you watched them suffer along with yourself in your mother's absence?" he asked.

"I don't think I would have even gone home if it wasn't for my sister and brothers," I said. "I wouldn't have been able to rest for worrying about whether or not they would be taken care of. Now I look at things in a different way, and I realize that we are a family who should love and support each other."

I could see Momma wiping tears from her eyes as I spoke. She was still holding my hand. I tried to hold back my tears, but I couldn't. Before I knew it tears were streaming down my cheek. I kept talking, though, and, as if on cue, Momma handed me a handkerchief. As I wiped my eyes I could see others in the room crying, as well! I cleared my throat and tried to speak as clearly as I could because I wanted everyone to understand what I was saying. My voice began to crack, but I kept talking. I looked at Momma and said, "Momma, we love you, and I thank God that I can face you and no longer feel angry with you for being an alcoholic. At first I was real angry. I was also confused and very disappointed with you. I thought you should have known better. It was very difficult for me to even look at you when you were drunk, because I no longer saw my beautiful mother. You looked and acted like a complete stranger to me. I felt like I had lost you for good. I know I have told you some of these things before, but never in front of anyone, but Momma, I now realize that you were hurting, and you needed help instead of me feeling angry and sorry for myself and blaming you. I now feel very proud to be your son. I'm also proud, Momma, in that you had enough courage to get help for your alcoholism, and I hope that you will stick with it because you're worth it, and you deserve all the happiness in the world."

Momma had the biggest smile on her face. The next thing I knew, Momma and I were hugging each other, and everybody in the room began to clap. I felt so happy, mainly because I could see my Momma taking control of her life again, and this made waking up in the morning worth facing. No longer did I feel bad about coming home. I turned toward Mr. Moore and told him that we all appreciated what he had done for our family in making sure that we got our lives back in order, and that if it weren't for him, I didn't know what would have happened to any of us.

The meeting ended with handshakes, hugs, and some admiration for certain individuals who had faced the biggest challenge of their lives—

alcoholism. I was also able to discover my own strengths and met new friends.

As we drove home from the meeting my mind drifted back to when I had been on the verge of giving up completely, until I was giving a new lease on life through the help of my buddy Patrick and Mr. Moore. I don't know what I would have done if it hadn't been for them pushing me forward with so many words of hope and encouragement. The highest honor goes to my heavenly father, because I knew that, with Him, all things were possible. I couldn't help but rejoice when I thought about my family—how we were growing together now instead of drifting apart. I felt as if God was watching over us every minute and helping us to be a little kinder and more patient toward each other.

I stayed out of school the next day because I wasn't feeling well. Instead, Momma had to get Willie and Aaron ready for school earlier than usual. Carmen was going over to Mama Rose's house. Momma came into the room after they left and asked how I felt. All I knew was that my throat felt like someone had stuck a hot iron to it and it hurt my whole neck, especially when I swallowed.

The first thing out of Mom's mouth was, "Jessie, I've told you over and over again about taking those showers every morning and going right outside into the cool morning air. It's a wonder you don't have pneumonia." She went on and on like a broken record. "And another thing, you need to stop walking outside in 40-degree weather with your shoes off. I can't understand you children. If you didn't have any shoes to wear, you'd be poking your lips out!" She stood before me with this stern look in her eyes. "Open your mouth, boy," she said. "I need to take your temperature."

Before I could open my mouth, she asked, "Jessie, have you been kissing on any of those fast little girls I see hanging around you and Patrick? I've heard some of them talk with their smart mouths, big eyes, ashy legs and all."

No way, I thought to myself. As far as I was concerned I had too many other things on my mind than to be bothered with girls. I shook my head from side to side. I wanted to laugh, but my throat hurt really bad. One thing I did notice, though, Momma was slowly getting back to normal. I didn't mind her fussing at me because I knew she was really concerned—her maternal instinct had surfaced, thank God. It made me feel like a little boy again, and it felt good!

Momma pulled the thermometer out of my mouth and said, "Yeah, you're running a fever, I opened up three cans of soup. You make sure you eat you some and drink some of that juice in the refrigerator, you hear me, Jessie?"

I smiled and said, "Yes, ma'am."

Before I knew it, Momma was kissing me on the forehead, then she said she had to go before she missed her bus for work. I had been lying on the couch and decided to sleep in Mom's room since her room didn't have as much sunlight shining through the curtains. I felt so dizzy as I walked toward her room; my throat hurt really bad. I only drank a little juice because it hurt so much when swallowing. I quickly plopped down on Mom's bed. I felt drained and exhausted, but for some reason I couldn't fall asleep. I stared into space, awaiting sleep; it didn't work. I figured if I counted the cracks in the floorboards, I would fall asleep.

I noticed something white sticking from up under Mom's dresser—usually there was a big throw rug right on that spot. I guess Momma must have washed it or something, I thought. I slowly sat up on the edge of the bed and walked toward the dresser. I bent down on the floor and slid my hand underneath the bottom of Mom's dresser until I had whatever the paper was in my hand. To my surprise it was sticking out of a thin book that I hadn't seen while I was on the bed—not only was it a book, but it read, "My diary," and Mom's name, Betty, was written on it. I know that diaries are supposed to be personal thoughts written for only the writer's eyes, yet I wondered about its contents and what Momma might have written on those pages. The diary looked quite old! I wondered how far back it went. I knew Momma must have really cherished it to hold on to it this long! I held the diary for a few minutes, then returned it but couldn't resist the temptation any longer—after about fifteen minutes had passed, I was back on my knees with Mom's diary in my hand. As I held it, I felt my heart beating as if I had been running, and I knew from the sweat popping off of my forehead that I was really doing something wrong, but I couldn't put the diary down. Some unknown force was causing me to want to read it—nosiness, I guess.

I was in too deep now to turn back or put it back. I slowly eased the paper out of the pages of the diary, since it was loose and sticking out I thought I would read it first. As I pulled it out, I saw that it was a letter. The paper appeared to be discolored and worn. My eyes quickly scanned the paper. I leaned against Mom's dresser—my illness suddenly made itself known again: dizziness momentarily overtook my curiosity, so I laid across the bed, all the while grasping Mom's diary and the letter in my hand. I pulled a pillow from the head of the bed and positioned myself comfortably on the bed. It was evident that any guilt I had about reading the diary was no longer a problem for me. As I laid across the bed I stared down at the letter on the bed. I slowly began to read, carefully savoring every word as if it were a meal and I wanted to enjoy every bite. In this case, I wanted to remember every word.

I began to read the letter. It read, "My dearest Betty, I know that you feel as if I have turned my back on you, but I haven't. I love you and I always will. Please try, if you can, to open your mind and heart to understand why I chose to go on to college. It's best for you and me in the long run. Betty, you of all people should understand that I was not prepared for what came from your lips a few months ago! I'm not blaming or pointing the finger at you for anything, because we both share a part in this unfortunate circumstance. Now we need to concentrate and work on the best course of action to take. Why don't you return my calls and stop dodging me? You're acting as if you hate me, and I know that you couldn't. I know that you're hurt and angry, and your anger won't allow you to answer my telephone calls. I'm hurt, too! Don't you know that I'm not proud of what has happened to us?

That's why I desperately need to talk face-to-face with you. I want to leave for college with a clear conscience in knowing that I have fully faced my responsibilities. I've already talked to my parents about our problem and was scolded at to the point of me wanting to just walk out of the door while they were talking and not come back. I thought my father was going to kick me out of the house that night, but he eventually cooled off after shouting himself hoarse. We had a long talk and came to an understanding on what was best for your sake and mine. Betty, please understand that, as I write this letter, I've had to drop the pen several times. I love you so much, and the pain of not seeing you hurts even worse. Why are you deliberately doing this to us? I never wanted our mistake to cause so many problems, yet we're dealing with one. Betty, will you please call me, see me or something? I'm begging you. Please, Betty. I do want to face my responsibilities, and do what I can to make your life easier, while I'm away at college. My parents promised me that they would not interfere, mainly because of your situation at home and knowing how strict your parents are and how your father wants an account of every move you make. When my dad told me I would have to talk to your parents, I froze up—your Momma doesn't frighten me as much, but your father, on the other hand, Betty, I have to admit I'm afraid to talk to him. I know your father is a fair man, but he has a temper like a short fuse. I think it would be best that you and I talk with him together. I know that you're afraid, but everything will hopefully smooth itself out. Time is moving on and you need to contact me before I leave town. Otherwise I'll have to come to your home again. This time, I won't leave if you dodge me by telling your parents that you are asleep or gone. Please call me, Betty. I miss you and I love you very much. You are very special to me and I only want you to be happy. Yours forever, J.L."

After reading the letter, I found myself more confused than ever. Who was this person writing to Momma? I didn't know of anyone with the initials J.L. Whoever the man was, he really seemed to care a lot about Momma. How he really felt, I guess Momma only knew that! Reading the letter made me want to read the diary even more. I quickly placed the letter on the bed and grabbed the diary. When I opened the diary, I saw that someone had written something on the inside cover of it. It read, "To our daughter Betty, on her 17th birthday. May you fill the pages with fun memories. Love, Mom & Dad!" I was not prepared for this. I began to get nervous. I'd always wanted to know who our grandparents were, but now I felt a little afraid, for some reason. I don't know why, but I felt relieved

LeNora Millen

because I didn't know how I would have reacted if Mom's parents'—my grandparents'—name had been signed on the cover of the diary. All I knew was their last name was supposedly Fremont, and that's the name all of us used. I quickly turned the page and read Mom's first entry in her diary.

CHAPTER 7

October 16-

Today was so special, because it was my 17th birthday. I know I'll never forget this day. I've had so much fun. I'm exhausted. Momma and Daddy had a very special birthday dinner for me at the church—all of my friends from school were there and I received the most beautiful gifts. I also met a new guy at church. His family just moved into town. I noticed him right off—he has the cutest smile and dimples as deep as the ocean. I could tell he was shy, because when I spoke to him, he smiled and looked down. I couldn't take my eyes off of him!

October 21-

On the way home from the grocery store, I saw him again. I waved and asked him how he was doing; he smiled and said, "Fine." He asked me whether I had a long walk home. Of course, I said I did, even though I was just a couple of blocks away. Before I knew it he was reaching for the bag of groceries I was carrying. He looked right into my eyes when I handed him the bag. I know he saw me blushing. He smiled and asked, "What do you have in here, a brick or something?" After we got to the house, I offered him a glass of water. "Thank you," he said as he reached for the glass. I made sure that when I handed him the glass, my hand touched his. I don't think I'll ever wash my hand again!

October 28-

I found out that he lives on Brilen Street. It's not far from home. I made a point to walk past his house on the way from school this evening—he was nowhere in sight. I felt like such an idiot. I walked up and down his street about three or four times. I know the neighbors were probably wondering who the strange girl was pacing up and down their street. I must be crazy or something, acting like this over a boy. I don't understand why I'm going all out of my way to see him. I don't know whether he even likes me yet. I think he does, but it could be my imagination. What if he's already dating someone? I've got to know before I fall flat on my face!

November 14-

He rode by my house today while I was sitting on the porch. He blew the horn and waved. Thank God he slowed the car down. He asked me how I was doing. I immediately jumped out of the chair and was headed down the stairs toward his car. I kind of leaned toward his window to get a glimpse of his cute face, then I told him that I couldn't hear what he was saying up on the porch, even though I could. What better excuse to use to get closer to him? "I asked you how you were doing. I hadn't seen you in a while. I just got back in town—you know how times flies," he said. "I'll be graduating soon and I've been visiting several college campuses, weighing the pros and cons of what they have to offer, before I make a final decision." All of a sudden I felt sad, I'm falling head-over-heels for this guy, I thought to myself, and he's leaving for college soon. I don't believe this crap; I put on a fake smile and asked him why he wasn't going to a local college. He said he would if they offered the courses he felt would be of benefit. So far, none of the local colleges compared to the ones he had visited with out-of-town. Then he said something that made me temporarily forget the thought of him leaving, "They may have a better curriculum to offer," he said, "but I didn't see any girls as pretty as you while I was there." He shrugged his shoulders and said, "Too bad!" We talked for a little while longer, but I couldn't stop thinking about the nice compliment he had given me. After he left I found myself daydreaming about him. Was that his way of flirting with me? I hope it was.

November 28-

I wonder what he did Thanksgiving Day. I couldn't stop thinking about him. He seems to be interested in me, but I can't really tell for sure. I don't want to scare him off by being too forceful, so I have been just smiling at him when I see him—no date so far. Why hasn't he asked me out? I can't take much more of this; if he doesn't ask me out soon, I'm going to ask him. I know I shouldn't, but I guess there's a first time for everything. At least I haven't seen him with anyone, but that's not enough proof—for all I know he could be dating someone at his school. Thanksgiving was really special, all the family was here, and of course, we had so much food we thought we were not going to have enough room in the refrigerator for it. I don't want to see another turkey, that's for sure—turkey and dressing, then turkey sandwiches, turkey salad, then turkey soup! I'm sick of turkey!

December 8-

You wouldn't believe what happened today—he finally asked for a date. I couldn't believe it, but I'm so happy, because I had lost my courage a few weeks ago to ask him. I still can't stop thinking about what he said. I've played it over and over in my mind, "Betty," he asked, "the Christmas dance at my school will be in a few weeks. I don't have a date, and I was wondering if you would like to be my date?" Yes, yes, my mind was screaming, but I kept silent, heart pounding and all as he spoke. "We've known each other for a few months," he said, "and I really enjoy being around you. I hope you don't get angry, but I had been asking around and found out you aren't seeing anyone. I didn't want to move in on someone else's girl. You aren't dating anyone, I was told. I hope that my information is correct," he said. "No, I'm not seeing anyone," I quickly replied. He said knowing I wasn't dating anyone made him feel a lot better, but that he was shocked that a girl as pretty as I didn't have guys knocking my door down. That is, until he found out how strict Mom and Daddy were. I laughed and said, "Now you know why," and that I would love to go to the Christmas dance with him, but he would have to ask my parents himself, because they would want to know firsthand who was taking me out. He smiled and said, "Okay, but do I have to wear a bulletproof vest?" I love his sense of humor. I hope after he meets Daddy, he'll still have one!

December 10-

Tonight, I thought I was going to walk a hole in the living room floor. I told Mom and Daddy that J.L. was coming over to ask their permission for me to go to the Christmas dance with him. Mom didn't worry me as much as Daddy. I knew Mom would be fair; Daddy, on the other hand, was so unpredictable. He made me want to run in my room and hide under my bed sometimes! When J.L. arrived, I ran for the door. Daddy, in his deep voice, said, "Sit down, girl, you act like you never saw the knuckle-head boy before." Daddy opened the door and stood for a few minutes, staring intently at J.L. J.L. smiled and introduced himself to Daddy and Mom. Mom smiled and said, "How are you doing, son." Daddy finally spoke after he had inspected J.L. from his head to his shoes and back to his head again. J.L. was so polite. I held my breath as he asked Mom and Daddy if he could take me to the Christmas dance. Before he could finish asking them if I could go out with him, Daddy started drilling him. He still had the toothpick from dinner poking from the side his mouth as if it were a cigarette. He gave J.L.

that serious look of his—that look where he tilts his head down and his eyes focus straight up. He looked like a bull charging after a matador, red cape and all. He asked J.L. who his parents were, where he lived, how old he was, did he go to church, did he work, was he going to college—you name it. It's a wonder he didn't ask him the brand of underwear he wore. I was so embarrassed. J.L. seemed somewhat nervous and amused at the same time. Mom sat quietly on the couch, and then she asked J.L. whose car he was driving. J.L. told her it was his dad's car. Mom asked him whether he had his driver's license. He told her he did. Her face took on a more serious expression and she told him that she expected us to act responsively and to keep our minds and hormones under control on our dates. She also asked J.L. to have me home by my curfew, which she would inform him of later. Daddy couldn't resist the opportunity—in an authoritative tone, he said, "Do your hear your Mom, Betty, keep them hormones packed away." He looked at J.L. and said, "You too young, man. We ain't raising no baby." Embarrassed by Dad's comment, I yelled out, "Oh daddy, you didn't have to say that." Dad snapped back, "I'll say what I want to. I pay the bills around here, not you, little girl, and don't you back-sass me." J.L., seeing my embarrassment, quickly said, "Sir, I understand, if she doesn't—my dad has told me the same thing." I thought I was going to scream. Daddy sure knew how to get his point across. What really made me angry was when J.L. got ready to leave. As I walked out on the front porch with him, I whispered in his ear so that Daddy wouldn't hear, and told him I was sorry if my parents seemed hard on him, especially Daddy. Before I could finish telling him this, Daddy yelled out, "I thought you already ate dinner, girl, what are you doing now, trying to chew the boy's ear off?" J.L. started laughing. He laughed so hard that he had tears in his eyes. He later told me to be thankful for having parents who love me and who want what's best for their daughter. Then, he jokingly said, "Betty, you haven't met my parents yet—they're probably as strict as yours. I've gotten angry enough to leave home at times, but if they didn't care, then I guess they would let us do anything we want, without asking questions." J.L. is so smart and mature for his age; there is something very special about him. After he talked to me I felt so much better. Before leaving, he leaned over and gave me a kiss on the lips, then said that he had to get home because his father needed the car! Daddy must have been peeping out of the curtains, because the porch light popped on like clockwork when J.L. tried to kiss me a second time. We burst out laughing, then J.L. said, "I believe someone is trying to tell us something. I'd better leave before I get you in trouble." After he drove off, I stood staring into the street until I could no longer see the back of his car. That night I slept like a baby. I'm in love; I'm really in love!

December 12-

I got a chance to meet J. L.'s parents. They seem to be very nice people. His mother picked out a beautiful corsage to match the dress I'm wearing to the dance. J.L. looks just like his dad. His dad seems like he's sort of quiet, but his mother talked my ears off, almost. She looks a living doll, she is so beautiful. She referred to me as "baby" the whole time, instead of Betty. I told her that I didn't mean to stare, but she that she was so beautiful, and that she reminded me of Lena Horne. His mom thanked me for the compliment; she said she admired Lena Horne's singing and acting and that her talent was also singing. Her dream, she said, was to be a famous singer one day. But after she met J.L.'s dad, she decided to settle down; instead she feels her singing voice is a gift from God, and is a part of her spiritual wellbeing. I asked her what she meant by that. She said she used to sing the blues, but now she sings for God. She said her soul is filled with God's love, and when she sings the spiritual songs, she is uplifted. Sometimes she says when she sings she becomes weak, and her knees start to shake, then she starts to feel faint, and before she knows it, the Holy Ghost uplifts her and helps her to stand. The words she sings, she said, engulf her soul, "And you know what, baby," she said, "it's as if the Holy Ghost is singing in my ear straight through my soul and out of my mouth." As J.L.'s mother spoke, her eyes sparkled, her voice trembled, then she began to sing. My God, I thought to myself, she has such a beautiful voice. The sound was unreal—never had I heard a sound so beautiful. I froze in the chair as she sang; her voice seemed to hypnotize me. Truly God had blessed her with a talent to sing, and she sang in his honor. Today was a very special day for me.

December 21-

J.L. picked me up for the Christmas dance tonight; he looked so handsome in his tuxedo. When he walked through the door, I found myself staring at him; he smiled at me and said, "You look beautiful, Betty." I was so nervous, I guess because it was my first date. When he pinned the corsage on me and kissed me on the cheek, I thought I was going to faint. Mom appeared out of nowhere, equipped with her camera, and took some pictures; she started to get emotional. She kept saying over and over again,

"Just look at my baby, she looks so pretty. It seems just like yesterday when I was changing your diaper. Now, look at how you've grown." Before I knew it she started crying. J.L. only stared, "Betty, you look beautiful," he said. He looked at Mom and said, "Mrs. Fremont, I'm proud to be her date. I'll probably be the envy of the dance." Mom said nothing, she just smiled, kissed me on the forehead and whispered in my ear for me to remember to act lady-like. I caught a glimpse of Daddy staring at me; he even complimented us by saying that we were a nice-looking couple. Lifting his big arms in my direction he told me to give him a hug. Daddy could be so gentle and affectionate when he wanted to be. J.L. shook his hand afterward and told Mom and Daddy that he'd have me home before my curfew. Daddy jokingly said, "Her and the dress—I paid a lot of money for that dress. I hope she remembers me coming to her rescue on her first date, because it emptied my wallet." Of course, we all laughed. I couldn't wait to get to the dance. This was a special night: my first date with a very special person whom I can't keep my eyes off of, and a smile out of this world!

LeNora Millen

December 22-

I had such wonderful time at the dance. I got a chance to meet some of J.L.'s friends. They were really nice, with the exception of one girl who kept staring at us, and giving me some wild-eyed angry looks. I asked J.L. who she was. He only laughed and said, "I only know her first name, Daisy. She's always staring at me. My friends claim she likes me. She's not my type: she acts like a weirdo or something. Don't pay her any attention, I'm with the person I want to be with," he assured me. By that time he asked me for a dance. As we danced he looked into my eyes and said that he was constantly thinking about me. He went on to say that he'd never been in a serious relationship, but he had feelings for me he didn't quite understand or know how to deal with. I found myself gazing into his eyes. He kissed me and whispered into my ear the words I will never forget. "Betty, I've never been in love, but I feel I'm falling in love with you. I've never felt like this about any girl. To tell the truth I've never really been interested." Then he started to talk with this funny accent. I think he wanted to sound like a Frenchman or something—the accent was hilarious. He said, "Betty, I want to be the prince charming in your life—your steady, as the older folks may say; your beau as the high-society folks would say; yo' man as the brothers say." He was too funny to be romantic. I couldn't help but to laugh, then he said, "Please say you'll be my girl," in this crazy-sounding voice. I laughed again and said, "Yes, I thought you would never ask. Your dimples won me over the first time I laid eyes on you." He hugged me so tight after I said yes that I couldn't breathe. It was evident that he didn't know his own strength. After we had danced several dances, my feet started to attack me with this horrible pain; the shoes seemed to be actually assaulting my feet. I can't describe the pain; all I know is that I had to get my feet out of those shoes, by any means necessary. I remember taking my shoes off that night, because it was hard to dance in them. The bottom of my shoes were also slippery, compounded with the fact that they were new and squeezing my toes like vice grips. J.L. saw me hopping and told me he'd carry me out of the dance before he would let me hop out. I hopped, anyway; I guess my pride got the best of me. When I got home I was exhausted and felt as if I had been running laps. J.L. and I said our goodbyes, and I undressed and charged for my bed. Mom and Daddy were still up. Thank God, I made my curfew!

LeNora Millen

December 25-

J.L. and I exchanged Christmas gifts with each other. He gave me this beautiful bracelet with three dove charms on it. He said the three doves symbolized love, peace, and joy—something he said our world lacked. The spirit of Christmas was in so many hearts; even Daddy was nice enough to give me some extra spending money to get J.L. a gift. I gave him a sweater. He tried it on and it fit perfect; he said he loved it. Later that evening, we went visiting family and friends and caught a movie. My last stop before going home was over J.L.'s parents' house. His Mom had baked several cakes and pies. She even sent two apple pies home to Mom and Daddy. I couldn't resist asking J.L.'s Mom to sing my favorite Christmas song, "Silent Night". Once she began to sing, we all joined in; her voice could soothe the wildest beast. The spirit of Christmas was definitely in the air and it felt good!

January 1-

The New Year came in with a boom! Daddy bought enough fireworks for just about the entire neighborhood. They were loud, but pretty to look at in the night sky! Earlier that night, all of us met at the church for a watch meeting, it was how we always started the New Year. J.L. and his parents were there, as a matter of fact; most of my friends and their parents were there, as well. Daddy and Mom were so funny. Daddy was continually asking Mom about whether she had remembered to turn the stove off. Mom had been slaving over the stove earlier that day and Dad knew that she was cooking his favorite—black-eyed peas. It was so funny watching those two bump heads with each other at the height of New Year's and their topic of discussion, black-eyed peas, of all things. I started laughing because I knew how passionate Daddy was about those peas every year. I interrupted the conversation and reminded Mom that she had indeed turned the stove off. Daddy, of course, made all of us laugh when he tried to whisper, but his voice echoed through the quiet church. Everyone there heard him say, "Well, I hope she turned that stove off, 'cause if those peas had burned, I was gonna be mad as heck." Dad looked around the church as he spoke, almost as if he wanted an audience. Mom had this look of embarrassment on her face as Dad rambled, "I want to start my New Year off right, in church, and with enough of those little black eyes in my mouth to make my soul fill rich, since I'm dirt poor. Mom hunched him and told him to stop pouting, and to thank God that he was alive to see another New Year upon us, and for him to also thank God for blessing him to be amongst his family and friends. We all prayed and gave thanks to God in our own special way. The New Year had a very special meaning for me. I looked upon it as a new beginning. Happy New Year!

January 12-

I've been too busy to write. My days and evenings are filled with much excitement and joy. I have so much to write, but so little time to do it, now that I'm dating J.L. The pages would go on and on if I started writing, so I guess I'll keep it short and simple, if I can. J. L. and I have a lot in common. I really love him, and I feel that he loves me. He's trying to decide what to do about college, at least decide where he'll be going. If I had my way I'd like him to stay close to home, but I know that his education is very important to him; so as hard as it is to do, I have to put my selfish feelings on the backburner. I'm also planning on attending college. J.L. and I know that securing a quality future won't happen with just a high school diploma. More good news—Mom and Daddy said that if I keep my grades up, they might buy me this cute little used car. I've had my eyes on this car for the longest. I promised them I would work hard on my grades. I can't wait to tell J.L. about the car. I feel my life has really taken a turn for the better.

January 20-

Today at church we had two baptisms: a husband and wife. It was touching to see them both being baptized. Afterwards the husband stood before the church and said that he and his wife had thought they had everything in their marriage. He said that they have a beautiful marriage, their own professional careers—he was an attorney and his wife, he said, owned a boutique. He spoke about their beautiful home, and their two beautiful children, but he said that there was a void in his life. He tearfully looked at the congregation and said that he walked around feeling this emptiness inside and couldn't figure out what was missing in their lives because neither one of them had been reared in homes where religion was emphasized. He said he felt that they had been led to the church by the grace of God. On the morning of the visit, the husband said that he could not go to sleep that night. Neither could his wife. He said he kept hearing the minister's words from his last visit at our church. He said he kept hearing the preacher's words, "Without God you're nothing; you may have all the material wealth the world can offer, but what does it profit a man if he gains the world and loses his soul." He said that as a result of the sermon on that fateful Sunday, he and his family would be members of our church family. I understand his testimony. I, too, have so much to thank God for, and he has blessed me over and over again. Thank you, God!

January 26-

J.L. and I got into an argument after church this morning. It was over a comment I made about our minister. I still don't know why he got so angry. During the sermon, I passed J.L. a note telling him to look at our minister's shiny bald head, how the reflection of the light bulb looked like a giant eyeball in the middle of his head. I also wrote that he preaches about the power of prayer—maybe he should pray for some hair instead of waxing his head to death! After church J.L. told me that I should be ashamed of myself for passing notes in church and making fun of the minister and taking God's worship in vain. I told him I was sorry, but that wasn't good enough for him. I got angry and told him that he's no Mr. Goody Two-Shoes, and he needs to quit trying to act like he's so perfect. He yelled at me and said, "I didn't say I was perfect, but at least I know how to act in church. You and your friends act so silly. I've heard the way you make fun of the church members' singing. "When Sister Booker falls asleep you're the first one to laugh, when she starts to snore," he said. He made me so angry, acting like he was so perfect. I told him that I didn't appreciate him acting like he was my father and that I didn't take orders from him. By this time Mom and Daddy were headed in our direction. I guess Mom could see from the expression on my face that something was wrong. She asked us if everything was all right. I said, "Ask Mr. Goody Two-Shoes." Mom looked puzzled, then she asked J.L. what was going on. J.L. looked at Mom and said, "She got the Devil in her, I guess." Daddy looked at me as if he could knock my head off, and said, "What's your problem, girl? Clowning out here at church. You know better; you look like you're mad at the world, and you need to stop poking your lips out. You look like a moose or something." Dad's comment really pissed me off; it wasn't fair for Daddy to side with J.L. before hearing my side of the story, I angrily thought to myself. J.L. burst out laughing at Daddy's remark. That did it. I jumped in our car and slammed the door as hard as I could. I was so angry with J.L. that I didn't even say goodbye when we left church, and I won't be the first one to call him, either!

January 28-

J.L. called me last night and I hung up in his face. I felt bad after I did it but I didn't want him to think that I was desperate for him, even though I missed him after just two days.

February 1-

No call from J.L. today. I guess he's paying me back or something for hanging up in his face. I definitely won't be the first one to give in. I did call him once today, but when he answered the phone I made a fart sound with my mouth in his ear and hung up. I couldn't resist the temptation. He's really got a lot of nerves. I'm over here feeling sad and he's answering the telephone like he's on top of the world. Who does he think he is?!

February 6-

J.L. and I made up; he picked me up for school this morning and apologized for being so judgmental the other day. It only took this remark to make me angry. J.L. tried to calm me down. He reminded me not to get angry when it came to him telling why we should give God our full attention in church. He suddenly leaned over, kissed me, and said, "Before you say something smart, I love you, Betty." I was speechless. I smiled and said, "I love you, too, J.L."

February 9-

Valentine's Day is only five days away, and I want to get J.L. something special. Daddy gave me some extra spending money since he knew I wanted to get J.L. a gift. Daddy's been so nice lately; I can tell he really likes J.L. Sometimes when J.L. comes to see me, Daddy ends up entertaining J.L. with these wild childhood stories that I've heard so many times I could repeat them as if I lived in Dad's time. On the other hand, J.L. seems to enjoy listening to Dad go on and on about his childhood escapades. I feel like the outsider sometimes, but I wouldn't have it any other way. I really love J.L. and it makes me happy to see him get along so well with my parents, especially Dad.

February 12-

It was so difficult deciding on what to get J.L. for Valentine's Day. I wanted to give him something that he could always remember me by. I want it to be something that will last, not be consumed in a few days or weeks, such as a box of candy, or a dozen roses whose beauty withers away as the days go by. It seems as if the female continues to get these same items each year. J.L. needs something unique or outside of the norm. After much thought, I decided to have the snapshot taken of J.L. and me at the Christmas Dance made into a portrait. Since I knew the artist and knew of his reputation as a good painter, it was an easy decision to make. He promised me that the portrait would be ready Valentine's Day! Upon picking up the portrait, my first glance of it left me speechless and emotional at the same time. I could only stare at it for a few seconds—the essence of the painting seemed to pull me within its canvas, and I honestly cannot find the words to describe it. I quickly turned and hugged Brian, ranting and raving at the same time about how lifelike and beautiful the portrait was. Brian stood proudly, with his chest upright and this big smile on his face. He never really talked much, and usually a smile, or blush. I guess he talked with his paintbrush and canvas. After paying Brian for the portrait, he covered it with a sheet and told me to handle it with care. "Who knows?" he said. "One day your children, if you have any, can boast about their mother having an original portrait painted by a then-struggling artist who made it big. You may be looking at the next Picassos." Having all the confidence in his God-given talent, I quickly replied, "You already have the talent, Brian. Now you must show the world what they're missing. One day your talent will be discovered, and you will then know in your heart that you are truly appreciated for your ability and insight to bring to life on canvas whatever or whomever you're painting." He smiled and said, "I hope so!" "You hope so," I responded. "I know so, and don't ever lose hope; hope is where we find our dreams and goals! And how we interpret those dreams is left up to how we direct our footsteps in life." I was sounding like my father, quoting him word-for-word. I went on, "We either strive with hope or become hopelessly extinct. This is what Dad always tells me, and I know that there's truth in this statement." I told Brian to always remember that God had blessed him with a talent that no one could take away from him. After thanking him again for the portrait, I left with a feeling of contentment! I knew that Brian would leave a mark in this world one day. I have my own original, my portrait of love, J.L. and myself.

CHAPTER 8

February 14-

Valentine's Day is finally here, J.L. picked me up from school today. When I got into the car he leaned over as usual and gave me one of his so-called original climb-the-wall kisses. I don't know what got in him that evening, but he thrust his tongue so deep into my throat that I almost choked on it. He looked at me with so much love in his eyes and said, "Happy Valentine's Day, baby." He kissed me again. Strangely enough, he had this wild look in his eyes I hadn't noticed before. He was really serious about something, for whatever reason. As soon as he kissed me I melted. When it came to J.L., he could charm the pants off of a pit bull. Before I knew it, J.L. grabbed my hand and placed a beautifully wrapped gift in it. I told him that I wanted to be the first to give the gift—"Ladies first," I reminded him. "What difference does it make?" he said. "I can wait, now stop talking and open your present." I quickly unwrapped the present. After taking the first glance at it, I remember screaming, "Oh my God!" My next words were, "It's beautiful, J.L." I couldn't believe it, J.L. had actually given me a ring, but what came next was the heart-stopper. His first words, with raised eyebrows, were, "Do you like it, Betty? I hope you do, because it took just about all my savings, but I know as my wife you'll pay me back in other ways—if you know what I mean." "His wife," I thought to myself. I felt almost like I was losing consciousness as he spoke. J.L. went on to ask me to marry him, with the understanding that we would have to complete college first, so I knew I was in for a long engagement. He went on to tell me how we would have to be patient with each other during the years ahead. He looked so serious. Abruptly he asked again if I would marry him, as if I wanted to suddenly back out. No way, I thought to myself. My mind was saying yes, but I couldn't get my mouth to move—this felt strange to me because I've always been a talker. I was never speechless or at a loss for words. Finally after recuperating from the shock of J.L. and I as husband and wife, I said I would marry him. I leaned over and gave him a kiss and hug so tight that I felt him gasp for air. I suddenly got emotional and started crying. There I was hugging this handsome hunk of man with mascara running down my face and on his shirt. I got so emotional that J.L. couldn't refrain from laughing. "Calm down, baby," he said. "Now I know you women can be sensitive at times. Here I am giving you an engagement ring as a token of

SEEDS OF DECEPTION

my love—you'd think I popped you in the eye or something the way you're carrying on." He laughed and said, "Now dry those tears, Betty. Save that for the onions you'll be chopping up when we get married." I thought to myself, "That's what he thinks—I can hardly fry an egg." After I came back down to Earth from J.L.'s proposal, I reminded him of the Valentine's present waiting at my house. Although nothing could outshine J.L.'s proposal, I felt he would really like my surprise. As soon as J.L. pulled into the driveway, I asked him to check his car for my bracelet in order to stall for time. This gave me a head-start on getting into the house. I wanted to get the portrait out of my bedroom before J.L. walked in. I nervously unlocked the front door and dashed toward my bedroom. I had a Valentine's Day card to give to J.L. along with his portrait, and I wanted to have the portrait hidden behind something and unveil it while J.L. read the card. Before I could get the portrait in the dining room, I heard J.L. coming through the front door; I immediately hid the portrait beside my bed. J.L. was soon calling my name. I yelled for him to have a seat in the dining room; instead, he headed toward my bedroom, asking me what I was doing. I don't know who was more nervous, J.L. or myself. J.L., looking around my room as if Daddy was going to jump from my closet, asked where Mom and Dad were. I told him that they had been invited to their friends' house for dinner. I could see from the look on his face that he felt sort of uncomfortable. I immediately wished him a happy Valentine's Day, and awkwardly leaned over and kissed him on his cheek. While J.L. read the card I walked over toward the side of my bed. I wanted to slip the portrait out before he finished reading the card. Instead, I tripped over the sheet covering the portrait and went headfirst into the wall. I don't know what hurt worse—my head or my integrity. I was so embarrassed. J.L. immediately helped me off the floor and onto my bed. He nervously asked me what had happened, and if I was all right. "I think so," I blurted out, after I explained to him what I was really doing. I slid the portrait toward him, still somewhat dizzy from the fall. J.L. looked puzzled and removed the sheet. His expression told me all I needed to know. "It's us," he said, with so much excitement in his voice. "I remember this all too well. We were at the Christmas dance." After staring at the portrait for a few more minutes, J.L. said, "Betty, I don't know what to say—this portrait will always be a part of my life because it has captured the person I love so much, your beauty, even on canvas it captivates the eye. This portrait represents us, Betty, our special bond, and I will always cherish it." He leaned over where I was lying and kissed me. I responded with a quick kiss. I felt sort of cross-eyed; J.L. must have noticed my expression, because he asked me whether I was feeling worse. I told him that my head felt as if it were going to explode. He asked whether he could get me some aspirin or an icepack for my head. I told him that I just needed to lie down for a few minutes, until my head stopped spinning. J.L. said that he would wait in the living room and watch television till I felt better, then said that he didn't want my parents coming home and finding him in my bedroom. I insisted he stay in my room. I told him it would be a while before Mom and Dad returned home. Hesitantly he sat next to me while I was lying down. Soon I felt myself nodding off. J.L. gently stroked my hair. He made me feel so special. He leaned over and whispered, "I love you, Betty," I felt his lips touch mine and I responded. J.L. kissed me again; the kiss sort of made me forget about my headache. J.L. suddenly snatched himself up. I don't know whether the fall took away my inhibitions—something strange was going on because I pulled him back towards me. I didn't want him to stop kissing me; it felt different to me this time than it had ever before. I felt this strange tingly feeling inside. My toes sort of quivered and my heart was pounding like a drum. J.L. grabbed the sides of my arms from around his neck and pulled away, then said, "Betty, we'd better stop while we're ahead." Innocently, I said, "All we're doing is kissing, J.L." He responded by saying, "It's not that simple, Betty." I wouldn't listen to him; my heart was saying something I hadn't heard before. I kept asking him to kiss me again; he was very hesitant at first, but soon relaxed. The next thing I knew J.L. was lying in bed next to me. I knew better, but I did nothing to stop what was happening. J.L. did try to stop, but I didn't.

March 20-

I'm so afraid, I think I might be pregnant. I missed my period this month. I don't know what I'm going to do if I am. Mom and Dad will be so hurt. As I write this I'm wondering whether to even tell J.L.. He'll be going off to college soon and I don't want to put a damper on things now that he seems so happy. I'm hoping I'm just late, even though at this point I may really be pregnant.

April 15-

I haven't felt like writing you much lately. There has been so much on my mind that I haven't been able to concentrate on anything outside of the baby that's growing inside of me now. August will be here soon. Today

I went over the community college to get signed up for my freshman year. While standing in line I got so nauseated that I had to run to the bathroom and throw up. It's been two—almost three—months now, and no period. I'm a nervous wreck. I took a home pregnancy test, and it confirmed my worst fears and what I already knew... I'm definitely pregnant. I don't know how long I can keep hiding the truth from my parents and from J.L.

April 16-

I think Mom is on to me. It may be just my guilty conscious, though. Today she asked me about me sleeping all the time, and why I'm staying locked up in my room so much lately. I told her that I just haven't been feeling well. She suggested taking me to the doctor. I immediately urged her not to by telling her that I had been just cramming too much. I lied and told her that I'll be okay. To make matters worse, I even lied on J.L. by saying that we had gotten into an argument and that I had been feeling down about it—that's why I'd been isolating myself. Mom, being her usual caring self, asked what the argument was about. I told her that it was over him and some girl he was flirting with. I hated lying to her, but I feel I'm living on borrowed time now.

April 28-

I've already made my mind up to tell J.L. that I'm pregnant. It's best that I tell him before I tell Mom and Dad; after all, he is the baby's father and he has a right to know. I'm so afraid, but maybe I'll get some comfort mentally by releasing some of the fear and frustration I've been carrying within me for months. Only God knows my innermost fears. Our sin could not be hid, even though I know my baby is not the sin, but the act committed by us was indeed sin. I can find comfort in knowing that I am truly blessed with loving parents with whom I've never been afraid to talk to about any problem. I'm too ashamed to look my parents in the face. Mom has always told me that she was against me engaging in sex, that I should try to wait until I was married or, old enough to understand my true emotions from hormones overreacting. Mom often said that there is nothing to be embarrassed about in being a virgin—purity is something to be proud of, she would say, and we should embody our entire spirit and soul with a presence of purity. This is what makes going to Mom so difficult—not because I fear my Mom (maybe Dad), but only because I feel as if all the long talks Mom and I would have about life in general, love, sex, marriage, you name it, all of the values instilled in me by both parents somehow got caught up in the moment of passion, and I let my weakness overrule my common sense. I know I'm only human, and I'm not perfect, but why am I so afraid? I guess it wouldn't be so difficult if I didn't have parents who have always been here for me through thick and thin, even though Dad sometimes comes across like the big bad wolf to some of my friends. I know the gentle heart he also possesses. He's always been sort of overprotective, sometimes a little too protective, but I know his actions are only out of love. I happen to be one of the blessed ones on this Planet who is fortunate enough to have parents who only want what's best for their daughter. Like Mom & Dad always say, no matter how old I am—even when I'm forty—I'll be their little pumpkin. I have so much respect for them, yet it appears that I've disrespected them in the worse way ever. Now I have to add tears to their eyes and pain to their hearts. Oh God, please help me, I never wanted to cause any problems for the two people I love most, yet I have.

May 12-

Today I called J.L. and told him I needed to talk with him about something very important. I guess from my tone of voice, he could tell something was wrong. He asked me if everything was all right at home. I told him all was well on the home front, but I didn't know how long it would last. Of course, he wanted to know what I meant. I told him that I would explain everything to him when he gets here. After J.L. arrived, Mom offered him dinner. I could tell by the way J.L. was acting that dinner was the last thing on his mind. It was obvious that J.L. was distracted and he wanted to talk to me and find out what was going on. He politely told Mom he'd already eaten, and that he really needed to talk with me. I hurriedly brushed past Mom and Dad, almost knocking Dad's newspaper out of his hand, at the same time asking Dad if it was all right if J.L. and I went to the park. Dad looked at me with that look of his he gives when he really wants to say no, but somehow he forced a yes out of his mouth. I didn't want to take any chances having Mom and Dad overhearing our conversation. I asked J.L. to drive me to the park because I always felt safe there—so many of my childhood memories were reawakened whenever I'd go there. Memories such as Mom pushing me back and forth on the swings, her smiling face with arms extended to catch me at the bottom of the sliding board, and the picnics I'd have with Mom and Dad almost every Saturday. I envisioned Dad throwing me up and down in the air, catching me so gently with his large hands, making sure I didn't hit the ground. My laughter could be found within the gentle breeze of yesterday and today within this park. My existence is captured amongst the trees rooted and grown over the years. As the seasons change and the leaves fall, life evolves over and over within the branches of the trees. Within the blooming of flowers, the sweetness of life's nectar had soured from my actions. In this paradise on Earth that holds so many memories for me, I, in a sense, corrupted its innocence by my weakness to my inner desires. I thought about Eve in the Garden of Eden and envisioned how Eve must have felt when she ate of the forbidden fruit. Now I find myself in a position where I tasted the forbidden fruit of my sin. Now a life is evolving within me and I stand here in shame before God and wonder what my punishment for my sin will be. My parents had taught me that Our Father in Heaven is a forgiving Father. I know this to be true, but I don't know how I can ever forgive myself. I've planted a seed of deception, and such, as the roots of the trees within the soil clinging on to each other for dear life, I'm also clinging. I know seasons change with a transformation man cannot truly duplicate; there is indeed life evolving over and over within these trees of carvings, past and present. With life being as a precious gem we should treat it as such. I silently asked myself who was going to be the one to polish my rough edges and smooth out my life, at this time it's in turmoil. J.L. 's voice broke through my wall of childhood memories, startling me for a second. He asked me what was going on. I told him I would tell him, but that I wanted to sit down first. A park bench was nearby so we sat down facing each other. I could feel my neck tensing up—this always happened when I got nervous. It was so difficult looking J.L. in his eyes and telling him I was pregnant, but somehow I mustered up enough courage to speak. I tried to find a right or proper way to tell him, but instead I blurted it out. I told him that I was three months pregnant and that I didn't know what to do and not to think I was trying to keep it hid from him. My silence, I explained, had only been because I had been so afraid. I told J.L. that I didn't plan for this to happen to either one of us, and that I wasn't trying to trap him into marriage or anything. J.L. didn't say anything; he just stared across the park as if he were trying to come up with an answer, but couldn't find one. He finally broke his silence and asked me why or how I could keep something so serious hid from him. He took a deep breath and said, "Betty, you let three months go by as if everything was fine, knowing we had a baby on the way." I explained to J.L. that I thought I might get my period, but I didn't, so I knew that it would only be a matter of time before the truth surfaced. I kept telling him over and over again how embarrassed and afraid I've been lately, but since my pregnancy is beginning to show I know I have to tell my parents. J.L. got up and walked from the bench. I remember him saying, "God, what am I going to do? One mistake and look what happens. We've only slept together once. I can't believe this." Looking quite disappointed, he said, "The both of us need to be there when you tell your parents." I told J.L. that I didn't want him there because I wasn't sure how my Dad would react. My reply seemed to only anger him. J.L. looked at me and said, "If I don't show up, your Dad will more than likely come looking for me, anyway. God," he said, "I can't believe this is happening, not now when I'm leaving for college. It's not that I can't support the baby, but the timing is so bad." I sort of got angry and told J.L. that he wasn't the only one who had plans—I'd had to deal with the stress of being pregnant, with being an unwed mother, and being ridiculed by society as a whole. I reminded him that I also had plans for college. He seemed to be only consumed by his own problems. I got angry and started crying, then I told him to take me home, and when I got ready to talk to my parents, I would be alone. I was so furious that I told him I didn't want him around when I spoke with my parents. J.L. frowned and said, "That's ridiculous. You know I need to be there, too, Betty; you need to stop acting like a child, you're going to be a mother now." I was suddenly speechless. Those words sort of played over and over in my mind—the words sort of hit me like a two-ton truck. Even though I know J.L. didn't really mean any harm, I took his remark like an insult. I remember bending down and picking up a handful of rocks and throwing them at him, then I clumsily ran toward his car, but not before I called him an insensitive jerk. After getting into the car I locked the doors. I was not going to let him in until I cooled off. I remember J.L. taunting me with remarks such as, "Look at her acting like a spoiled brat." Then he said, "I hope it makes you feel good locking me out of the car, but one thing you forgot, Miss Know It All, I'm the owner of this car." With this smirk written across his face, he reached in his pocket and pulled out his keys, swinging them back and forth in the air. At that point I wanted to break his wrist. I remember rolling my eyes at him until I got a cross-eyed headache. J.L. didn't say anything at all to me on the way home. After J.L. pulled in front of the house, he didn't even look my way. He just stared straight ahead, then said, "I'll call you later, because the both of us need to talk to your parents." As sensitive as I was I got angrier and said, "This child, or brat as you referred to me as being, doesn't need you to babysit her when she tells her parents she's pregnant. I can handle it myself." I remember my voice getting louder. I looked directly in his eyes and said, "You can take your high-falutin' attitude back home, preacher boy." I don't know what got into me, but I lost it. I took the engagement ring off my finger and threw it at J.L. I told him he could take his ring back, then I called him a phony who only pretended to love me. I told him that I didn't want to interfere with his college plans, and that I didn't want him to feel obligated, if he knew what I meant. I know I said a lot of things I probably shouldn't have. I even tried to stop myself, but I couldn't. J.L.'s facial expression showed hurt. I was hurting, too, but I didn't know any other way to respond. I remember feeling like my world was crashing down around me. I dreaded facing Mom and Dad, and even though I love J.L. with all my heart, I felt a need to push him away. I'm so confused. I really can't explain why the people I loved more, I felt a need to reject them. It seems like it's easier to deal with it that way. I felt that by putting up a wall around me and not letting anyone penetrate it, I would be safe. Deep in my heart I knew this wall was only a façade, for I was really trying to hide within myself. I wanted to really crawl into J.L.'s lap and cry like a baby, and I really wanted to fall into Mom and Dad's arms and cling for dear life, yet another person was emerging within me, a person I feel I'm not really familiar with. I seem to be losing control.

May 15-

J.L. has been calling me on a daily basis, I'm not ready to talk to him, so I feel it's best not to return his calls. Mom & Dad are really concerned with what's going on between us. I really love J.L., and giving him back the engagement ring, I know, is probably one of the biggest mistakes I'll ever make. I don't really understand what's happening to me. Somehow I feel as if my life is taking a turn over which I have no control. Or do I?

May 18-

J.L. called today while Mom and I were out shopping. He even had enough nerve to ask Dad whether I had talked to them about a personal matter between us. Dad said he told J.L. that I had only talked about us breaking up. Dad started to almost interrogate me, by telling me about a conversation he and J.L. had earlier that day. I pretended that I didn't hear. Dad kept talking, then said that J.L. told him that I wasn't being completely honest with him about us splitting up, and that it had not been his choice to call off our engagement. Dad looked at me with his eyes focused directly on mine and said, "Baby girl, J.L. tells me that it was your idea to split up and that you wouldn't even listen to him when he tried to talk some sense into that stubborn head of yours." Dad seemed really concerned with my situation and told me that he could hear the hurt in J.L.'s voice when J.L. told him he still loved me and would never do anything to hurt me. Dad also said that J.L. told him he felt he needed to talk to them face-to-face. I couldn't believe J.L! The nerve of him! And to make matters worse, it looked like Dad was taking his side. It was not my imagination; he was even looking upside my head, rolling his eyes like I had committed a crime or something. Dad talked to Mom and then said that if I didn't tell them what was really going on, they would both call J.L. and have him come over, whether I liked it or not. This really ticked me off. Here I am, their daughter, and they're threatening me. I remember jumping up off the couch and screaming to the top of my voice, "Go ahead, call him. I don't care anymore about what happens." For the first time ever, Dad was speechless. He stood up as if he wanted to grab me and shake my eye sockets out or something, but he didn't say anything. He just looked at me with his hands on his hips and this question mark-like expression on his face. His mouth was hanging wide open, but nothing came out of it. I knew then I had to make a run for it before anything came out of his mouth or the shock of me screaming at them wore off. I took off running toward my bedroom, quickly locking the door behind me. Mom was soon at the door knocking and shaking the doorknob, frantically asking me to unlock it. This went on for about ten minutes. I finally unlocked the door; once Mom entered the room I waited on her to scream, yell… whatever. I just wanted it to be over with; instead, she grabbed me and held me as tight as she could, then she said she loved me before saying anything else. She told me that whatever was bothering me that nothing was so horrible that I couldn't talk to her about it. Mom reminded me of all the things we've shared together, and of all the talks we've had about God-knows-what. She looked at me and said, "Baby, when did your mother become a stranger to you? You've always told me I was your Rock of Gibraltar, and that there was no problem we couldn't handle together." She had tears in her eyes, then she said, "Betty, you're at the point in your life when you need a rock to lean on; it's not fair for you, or anyone for that matter, to carry the weight of life's problems completely alone." Mom reminded me of one of her favorite poems, "Footsteps in the Sand." She held me tight as she whispered these words, "You were never alone, I was there carrying you all the time. This is what the heavenly father has been doing for you all this time." "Betty," Mom said, "you just never took time to realize his grace." Mom told me to put my faith in God and things would work out, then she asked me to tell her the truth about what was really going on with J.L. and me. When I opened my mouth to speak I couldn't get the words out; I remember crying so much until I felt I couldn't anymore. I begged Mom to let me tell her and Dad tomorrow. Mom hesitantly said, "We'll wait until tomorrow, but no later." I know within my heart that tomorrow will be a day I don't want to face, my day of reckoning has made its fateful appointment.

May 19-

Today was a day I know I'll never forget. I was finally faced with telling Mom & Dad the truth. I will never forget the expression on their face when I told them I was pregnant. Mom dropped her face within her hands and said, "Oh God, no, not my baby." Daddy jumped up from the chair he was sitting in and yelled out, "You're what?!" Mom grabbed his arm and told him to settle down. Everything looked like it was happening so fast. Mom kept telling Dad to let me explain to them what happened. After Dad finally calmed down, after gritting his teeth to the point of making my skin crawl, I was faced with telling them what started out as the truth, but somehow this other person evolving within me took over. It was as if I allowed this unknown being, making itself known within me, steer the words right out of my mouth. I remember telling them that J.L. and I had slept together one day when they were not home. Daddy interrupted me and said, "You mean 'had sex,' don't you?" I tried to ignore his remark, but snapped back, "Yes, Dad, we had sex." Mom asked whether it was my first time with J.L., and whether there had been other times. I didn't answer at first, then I told her that J.L. and I had only slept together once. Daddy said, "Only once, huh, here under our roof. After all we've taught you, you would still disrespect us that much." To add more anguish to his remark, he gave me such a look of disgust. He stood tall like a soldier preying on his enemy, sucking the side of his teeth as if he had just eaten a steak and was trying to suck out the rest of what was left. I felt myself getting angry, all the while trying to keep this other being within me from losing control. Mom looked at Dad and asked him to let me explain. Daddy interrupted Mom and said, "Explain what? How she had sex here? What more does she need to tell us?" I started crying and told him it wasn't planned and how I had tripped and hit my head, but before I could finish he interrupted again by saying,

"Your head wasn't hurting too much to open your legs like some cheap tramp, now was it?" That did it. I found myself losing it. I tried to stop what was happening, but I couldn't. I heard myself saying, "Yeah, Dad, I guess I am a tramp. Maybe I'm a sex addict or something." Mom was shocked. She angrily looked at me and told me to stop talking like that to Dad. It was too late by then; I told her and Dad that the reason I didn't want to tell them I was pregnant by J.L. was because I didn't think that J.L. was the baby's father. Dad leaned over toward me and yelled, "What in the Hell do you mean, girl? You just told us a few minutes ago that it was you and J.L.'s first time." I angrily snapped back, "I know what I said. It was our first time, but I had been with other guys before him." Mom looked on with so much hurt in her face she had tears streaming down her cheeks and she was shaking nervously. I wanted to run over to Mom and tell her that I was afraid. I wanted to apologize to them both, but I didn't. Instead, I played a role I will never win an award for. Dad asked again, "What other guys are you talking about, Betty?" I told him he didn't need to know. I had started a lie that I almost believed. Dad looked at Mom and said, "Do you hear our daughter? She's sitting here in our living room making light of the fact that she's pregnant, and that J.L. may not be the father, and that she's been sleeping around with God-knows-what." Mom's voice cracked as she spoke. She looked at me and said, "Is this the truth, Betty?" I looked down because it hurt me too much to look her in the face, and said, "Yes, it's true. Like Dad said, you have a tramp for a daughter." Mom angrily said, "Stop referring to yourself as a tramp. You know that J.L. loves you and the right thing for you to do is not deceive him, but tell him what really been going on with you. I know he'll do right by you." I told Mom that she was too trusting and naïve, that J.L. was like any other man who only wanted an easy lay and he got one and that I was three months pregnant now. Then I said, "Isn't life full of surprises? While he'll be going off to college, I'll be preparing myself for motherhood." I told Mom and Dad that I didn't want J.L.'s sympathy and I didn't want him feeling obligated to a baby who might not even be his. Daddy walked over to me and grabbed the bottom of my chin in his hand. He looked me directly in the eyes and said, "Listen, little girl, if you keep this funky attitude you got along with this newfound arrogance I'm seeing in you, you'll never amount to anything in your life. You can walk around here with your head stuck in the sand like an ostrich if you want to, with your butt stuck up in the air for every Tom, Dick and Harry you meet. Remember this, little girl—no man will ever respect you unless you respect yourself. When I called you a tramp I didn't literally mean you were one. I only spoke out of anger, and I apologize for that, but I don't apologize for being your father and wanting what's best for you. Neither does your mother. It seems that, from your own admission, you want to be a tramp, or are you just bluffing. You see, I know you all too well, Betty. I know that you're really frightened and you're putting on this brave little front, but deep inside you're hurting like hell." He was telling the truth, but I had to keep focused. I had to keep the lie I had set into motion going. Somehow I just didn't care anymore about what was happening. All I wanted was for everyone to leave me alone—that meant Mom and Dad as well as J.L. I lied and told Dad that I wasn't afraid and that I knew exactly what I had done. I told him that I tried to be the daughter he and Mom wanted me to be, but couldn't; and if they couldn't accept me as I am now, then they were up for a lot of disappointment. Mom, still shaking her head in disbelief, asked about J.L. and how he was dealing with the situation. I told her that J.L. was past tense with me; that I still loved him, but life goes on and that I wasn't going to sit back and wait on him, or any man, for that matter. Dad looked at me sort of disappointed, and said, "Girl, the boy is willing to marry you. Stop talking like some primitive fool." I told Dad that I didn't want to marry J.L. and asked them if they were ashamed of me, being that I'm unwed and pregnant. They said that they were not, but I knew they were only pretending. I knew they would feel better if J.L. and I married, because that would alleviate embarrassment for them. I wondered if they even thought about the silent pain and anguish I'm going through. I even put myself in a position in their eyes as if I was some cheap slut who slept around. For what? I have nothing to gain. Surely I've lost the respect of those dear to me. All I know is that I've got to leave here as much as it hurts me. I know I can't stay here much longer. Yes, I am afraid, and I have all these mixed emotions surfacing within me. I know that lying to the most important people in my life is not the answer. Sometimes the truth isn't even the answer, even though the truth is always best. I have to do what I have to do. My life at this point will never be the same. The most frightening part is the simple fact that I don't know what's in store for me. My parents are truly wonderful people. I love them dearly, but I've hurt and deceived them. I've also hurt J.L. and I know his parents will be disappointed, as well. Now I have to focus on the baby growing within me. I don't think I can ever look Mom and Dad in the face anymore, as I've done before. Oh God, what have I done? I know this lie will someday come back to haunt me, but how? It's time for me to move on, but where am I going to go? And how am I going to support my baby? One thing I do know is that this is, indeed, J.L.'s baby; and if this baby is anything like J.L., he'll make me proud someday, but will I lose a son or daughter because of my deception? I pray that God forgives me for what I'm doing. The irony in all of this confusion that I have created is that I will have a part of J.L. with me wherever I go. I know that J.L. will be hurt, but hopefully time will heal his pain with the months and years to come.

CHAPTER 9

This was the last entry in Mom's diary. I actually felt as if I'd stepped back into Mom's past and relived the joy, the pain, and the fear she described in her own words as best as she probably could. I found myself laughing at some of the things Mom had written about, especially when she described her father, the patriarch of the family. My grandfather, a serious man who also seemed to possess a witty sense of humor. A grandfather I'd always wondered about, yet only being allowed the stolen glimpses of him through the mental images within my mind. My grandfather was described by Mom as a strong-willed, proud man who loved his family; a man who didn't bite his tongue when it came to his true feelings; a man who embraced life realistically and cautiously—his main objective being that he wanted to protect the sanctity of his family; a man who had to face the struggle of confronting the daughter he loved dearly, only to be betrayed by the innocence of her own guilt. My grandmother seemed to be the balance in the family—the peacemaker, of sorts—a grandmother who was described by Mom as being a very soft-spoken and spiritual woman. Grandparents we could never ask about; grandparents never seen; yet I discovered these unmentionable grandparents through the worn, faded pages of Mom's diary. There were also tears, many tears. Reading abut the unpleasant experiences Mom had struggled through, especially when she couldn't deal with being pregnant with me and describing herself as feeling so confused that she would turn her back, not only on her own parents, but the man she professed to love—J.L., my father.

Reality had really begun to set in and I had to deal with the facts before me. Still weak from my illness and clutching the diary to my chest, I held on to this little black book for dear life. Without a warning, I felt the rush of adrenaline throughout my body; I would soon feel tears beating their way through my eyelids with the force of tidal waves. My entire body seemed to open up in order to release the pain within. I opened my mouth to let go of some of my anger by screaming, but nothing came out. Instead my body only trembled and I began to cry uncontrollably. I felt as if I was crying the tears of the grandparents I never knew. I cried the tears of a father who was not allowed to know me as his son. I cried the tears of a son who was stripped of a father, not by his own choice, but by a mother who really didn't know how to deal with life's struggles, a mother who made a choice out of deception, leaving a trail of pain behind her; and somehow this same pain seemed to have found its way within the core of my heart, slowly ripping apart the essence of my whole existence. I was quickly consumed with more anger and more tears.

After crying uncontrollably for several minutes I found myself lying on my back, staring blankly at the ceiling. The sound of the water dripping from the faucet in the bathroom seemed to bring me back to whatever level of consciousness I had left. I knew Mom and the others would be home soon, so I had to be sure and put Mom's diary back in its rightful place. Still dizzy from my illness, I felt my body slowly lift up off of the bed. I was soon kneeling in front of Mom's dresser as I had when I first discovered the diary, only this time I was returning it.

As I slid the diary back within its dusty hiding place, I felt more like I was leaving my soul within those pages. Before leaving Mom's bedroom, I remember standing in the doorway with a newfound sense of who I really was. I knew that I was not the same person who had entered this room earlier that morning. Within a matter of hours I was reborn, in a sense, by the written seeds of deception throughout the diary's pages. My identity was no longer that of a young man whose existence came without the foundation of the ever-extinct black father. This new feeling of knowing that there was a man, described as my father, who was willing to extend love and take on the responsibility of being a father, gave me a sense of pride that I'd never really known or felt. Knowing that I was not just another young man or unwanted statistic through the heat of passion empowered me. I soon began to feel an urge to seek out my father, a man known only to me as J.L.. Where the search would begin, God only knew, yet I was suddenly hit by the unpleasant thought of him not accepting me as his son. I even wondered if he were still alive, and, if so, whether Mom's deception had caused him to become a bitter person or whether he had even tried to locate us. Only a few days ago I had been on top of the world. I had struggled and watched my family be pulled in so many different directions, but we had never given up hope. We all somehow dealt with the pain of those struggles, and through the grace of God were able to reshape our lives, in a sense, to overcome some of the hurt and pain we had endured. Of course the emotional scars existed within us, but with time and patience, hopefully, we'd continue to conquer the pain and find, within each of us, the joy we all rightfully deserved.

My mind soon drifted to Mom's alcoholism; her struggle with her drinking was definitely a turning point in her life. Thank God Randle was no longer around to harass her; he was partially to blame for Mom's drinking. He had taken Mom on an emotional roller coaster ride to Hell and back. Now he was behind bars for life for shooting a man simply because the man didn't give him money to buy drugs. I shudder to think it could have been one of us. That's why I never took Randle's threats as him just talking—he meant what he said when he threatened to kill all of us without blinking an eye. That ugliness was behind us now. Mom was finally able to get help for her alcoholism and regain her sense of self again—more importantly, to love and respect herself.

Things had really gotten better around here. Now I was being hit with this! I should have just left the diary where it was, but it was too late to talk about what I *should* have done; the fact was that I *did* read the diary and I must deal with what I know even though I didn't know, at that point, how. I'd tried to make sense of everything. I should have been happy, but why was I so confused? All of these mixed emotions within me were causing me to think irrationally. I'm no different than any other person who would probably be feeling the same pain I was feeling; moreover, a feeling of betrayal.

As I returned to my room, I fought back more tears, and tried to come to terms with the anger I felt towards Mom. I knew I had no right to judge or condemn her for what she had done, and I knew she really hadn't meant to hurt me. I truly believe she only wanted to protect me in the only way she knew how. God, if I ever needed strength, it is now. At that point I didn't really know how to deal with what I knew. In a few weeks, I was supposed to be baptized. This was supposed to be one of the happiest days in my life, but somehow my happiness had been shattered without warning. I'd been waiting patiently waiting on Mom to regain her courage to enter the church. I didn't quite understand her reason for not wanting to mention God or church. I now understood that she had cheated herself in the true fulfillment of God's love. So many thoughts were running through my mind. I fell across my bed feeling as if I were carrying the weight of the world upon my shoulders. It was not long before I started drifting off to sleep.

When I woke the next morning I didn't feel as sick as I had the day before. Willie and Aaron came running into the bedroom, both taking turns giving me their own special hugs. As I hugged them I began to think about Mom's dairy and what I knew. It felt good seeing their smiling faces, with so much love reflecting in their innocent little eyes—both of them wanting to know how their big brother was doing. It was evident, as always, that they were competing for my attention. Each one came with their own special charm and gifts. Aaron gave me his favorite bag of marbles. I knew as soon as that little joker got angry with me, he'd be asking for them back. Willie gave me a lollipop he said he'd found in his dresser drawer. It was sort of comical watching him stick out his chest proudly, saying, "Jessie, I hope it still tastes good. I think it's been in my drawer for about two years." Aaron started to laugh and told Willie that he'd given me sissy stuff, then he told Willie that a real man likes marbles, not some old stale sucker. Looking for my approval, he said, "Ain't that right, Jessie?"

Still somewhat emotional from yesterday, I grabbed the both of them in each arm, fighting back my own private pain, and told them that it didn't matter so much about what they gave me because I knew that they both loved me and that's what's important. I had to stop and clear my throat as I spoke, because my voice was still very scratchy from the cold. I told them that being thought about really made me feel a lot better.

Their response wasn't what I expected. They both burst out laughing, but not before telling me that I sounded like one of the cartoon characters they'd watch on television. Little Carmen wasn't to be left out of the excitement; she ran into my room with her favorite doll fastened in the grip of her tiny fingers. She crawled up next to me and gave me one of her sloppy kisses on my cheek. I smiled and asked her what she and her little doll were up to. She shrugged her shoulders at first with an "I don't know" expression written on her face, then she said, "Dollymae and me were talking this morning about you."

I humored her and said, "You were? Well, I hope it was something good."

Carmen flashed a big smile across her face; she looked so funny since she'd lost her two front teeth. She batted her long eyelashes and said, "Dollymae and I have to make sure you get better because we want to hurry up and see you get capsized at church."

I laughed and said, "Who told you I was getting capsized?"

Carmen smiled and said, "Willie and Aaron told me you were going to get capsized—that's who told me." Leave it up to Willie and Aaron to come up with their own definitions. I had to be careful with my answer. I didn't want to confuse her anymore than Willie and Aaron had already. I told her that when she comes to church, she'd see what I'd be doing and that maybe one day when she was old enough to understand it, she might experience the same thing.

Carmen sort of gave me a puzzled look, then said, "What about Dollymae? Can she be capsized?"

Before I could answer I saw Mom standing in the doorway with a smile on her face; my eyes immediately fastened themselves to the floor. Then she spoke, "How you doing, Jessie? When we got back last night you were knocked out. I didn't want the kids to disturb you, so I told Willie and Aaron to sleep on the couch. As for Carmen, well, you know where little Miss Busybody slept."

I only stared at the floor. Mom asked again whether I was feeling better and walked in the room. I responded quickly and said that I felt better than I had the day before, but that I wanted to be left alone because I had a terrible headache. She reached toward my head as if to see whether I felt warm. I immediately pulled away and told her that I just needed to rest. I turned my back toward her; this was my only escape I felt I had during that time.

Mom, in a concerned voice, asked me if I wanted some juice or something to eat. I whispered, "Mom, I'll be fine. I just need to be alone right now." She looked worried, then told Carmen to let me rest. Carmen begged to stay until Mom told her she might catch my cold and have to get a shot. Carmen hated the word "shot"; she hated needles even more, and was out of the room in a flash. Mom shut the door behind her after asking again if I needed anything. I was left alone to struggle with confused feelings and a mom I didn't want to push over the edge.

As the days and weeks passed by, the anger within me also passed. I had put off my baptism several times because I had to deal with getting my mind cleared up from some of the anger I had been experiencing. I was also trying to deal with not blowing my lid when I would sometime get the urge, especially when Mom would get on my case about something. I came close several times to just letting her know exactly what I knew and telling her about the private hell I'd been living with. Only through prayer was I able to mellow my heart, enabling me to somehow forgive Mom instead of harboring the resentment I had felt. I was also able to take the negative I projected toward Mom and turn all those angry negative feelings into something positive. Although it was difficult, somehow God put a protective arm around my family and held us together. I, being the foundation, couldn't crumble, because I knew my actions would have torn down the very fabric of the family structures we all had worked so hard to pull together. We were all like links in a chain being held together, and the links were very fragile. Even though the love between us was strong, it was going to take more than love to keep our chain from breaking; it was going to take understanding and forgiving; it was going to take patience; and, most importantly, it was going to take faith.

With this newfound understanding spawned by consistent prayer, I knew that Mom would have the struggle of her alcoholism to deal with for the rest of her life. I had enough faith to know that she'd be victorious—she was not fighting this battle alone, and she'd actually come to know a higher power through the counseling program she was in. I'd seen a change in her I never would have been able to imagine.

Prayer also had changed things for the betterment of my family. It has opened my eyes and heart to see that my mother made some choices in her life that she herself had suffered for as a result of those choices. Through the pain and agony of her alcoholism, she'd struggled to regain her dignity and her own self-worth, and she was truly focusing on staying sober. Who am I to pass judgment on her? And who am I to take those skeletons of Mom's past and condemn her as if I were the almighty? I knew that I had not been born into this world to cause my mother to lower her head in shame for her choices or mistakes, and I was not to cause my mother to shed more tears or inflict more pain in her heart.

At that point, I didn't know the road or choices I'd make in life; I could only hope and pray that if I was faced with the unknown or hidden secrets, I prayed that I would be strong enough to withstand the things life might dish out. I prayed that if I did become weak and succumb, that I'd somehow regain the strength and steadfastness to face my problems head-on and not become a victim of my own fears or blame others for my own mistakes. It's true also that I didn't have a choice in my existence, but the fact is that I do exist, and I can't use the excuse I didn't ask to be born for the rest of my life, especially now that I knew that I had a choice in the paths taken. I chose to be that positive light that shines in the heart of mankind; I chose not to boast so much about what I was going to do, but let my actions be my illuminator of hope.

I was also clinging on to the hope that my entire family would someday follow the path of righteousness and be baptized one day. It was a blessing to see how my family's lives had taken a turn for the better. I'd always heard that God works in mysterious ways, and I saw that God had worked with my family. I'd always looked at my best friend Patrick as one day being this fireball preacher, but for whatever reason God seemed to have directed us into each other's lives and directed me to preach his word someday.

The most ironic part in all of this was that I seemed to be following in the footsteps of the man I had read about in Mom's diary—my father J.L. All the pieces of my life were somehow being put together such as a puzzle. Sometimes a piece might get misplaced or temporarily forced into a place where it really didn't belong, but with time and patience the pieces of our life's puzzle would soon fall into place. I couldn't say at that point if I'd ever let Mom know that I had read her diary, but I felt in my heart that when I did, it would be done with love. She'd been hurt enough.

I also had to concentrate on Willie and Aaron. Gangs were sprouting up all over the place, and being threatened myself by these gang members, had put enough fear in me to know that it was going to take a lot to keep them from being influenced. I knew that fear was what crippled so many of us, and the residue of this same fear had left its blood-stained marks throughout the fabric of my neighborhood and society as a whole.

I often wondered if we as a people and community, ever took time to ask ourselves whether our fears were justified. Were we guilty of giving in to our own self-destructive weaknesses and using this crippling crutch of fear as an excuse? I'd seen some in the neighborhood appear to close their eyes to what was really happening within their homes. They would simply give up and say, "It's not my problem." When this happens we, in turn, are openly saying we don't care, as long as it doesn't affect us. In the long run, we all suffer. When will we as a people begin to conquer our fears and strategically move forward in a positive way? This is the beginning of wisdom and growth. We have to love ourselves more; therefore, we can begin to overcome our own appetites of self-destruction.

My mind was so full. There was so much I felt I had to do, but I didn't know where to begin. The most important thing in my life was the desire for my family's safety. I'd do what I had to do to keep them from harm, even if I was confronted again by the gangs, I'd have to do what I could to survive. If I could help one gang member turn his or her life around, that would be one life spared. The saddest part of this scenario was that they felt protected by those individuals they referred to as their family, but for how long? Many would eventually have a bullet with their name written on it if they chose to remain in the gangs, eventually becoming another statistic. How could they allow their lives to be taken from them for nothing more than an angry look, the wrong colors, turf protection? Their own fears for protection would manifest into a deceptive protection of eternal doom.

I talk to Willie and Aaron as much as I can about not being forced to join gangs. I tell them to not let fear keep them from talking to me, even if my life is threatened; I've made a point to let them know that their lives are too precious to risk. If it means telling them every day, I will. I have come to the realization that when just one person's life is taken, the cry within our communities should be heard. These sorrowful wails as they echo throughout our neighborhoods should forever remain on our conscience to remind us that someone is left with emptiness inside. They can be heard asking over and over, why? Why my husband, my wife, my child, my sister, my brother, my friend? Again they ask, why did this happen? Only then do some of us call upon our heavenly father and bury our face in our hands and pray! Lest any of us forget that God never left us—we turned our back on him.

Even though Willie and Aaron may not yet fully understand God's power, I continually tell them that it is the wisdom from God that inspires me. This wisdom will hopefully be shared with all ages; God's grace is ever-present and is now upon our household.

Before I went to sleep, I prayed to God that he'd continue to watch over my family. I also prayed that, if it was God's will, that I might someday meet J.L., the father I had discovered in Mom's diary. After giving thanks to my heavenly father, I got in bed. I was exhausted—more mentally than physically.

For the past few weeks I'd had so many things on my mind: my baptism, Mom's diary, and how I'd felt sort of unbalanced. Mom even noticed me staying more to myself and locking up in the room. I told her that I was just tired and needed to rest. After getting into bed, I finally felt myself slowly drifting off to dreamland; it had started to rain, so I knew I would be soon asleep. When I was younger it would rain and I would listen to the raindrops hitting the windowpane and side of the house and fall immediately to sleep. The sound of the rain seemed to soothe and cradle me. Sometimes it sounded like the raindrops fell with a rhythm. The sound of the thunder I imagined to be drums beating to the rhythm of the rain. I guess that's why thunder never frightened me. My imagination as a child was one thing that helped me to survive the nightmares of the past.

After awaking, I felt tired and confused. I remembered having the moistness of tears in my eyes; I'd dreamed the strangest dream, which left so many unanswered questions in my mind. In the dream I remembered hearing someone call my name, but for some reason when I answered no one answered back. As far as I knew, I was asleep in my room when I heard my name being called again. I got out of bed and remember looking around, but saw no one. I heard my name being called once more, so I stepped out into the direction the voice was coming from. When I got in the hall it turned into a road—a long, foggy road. I was scared because I didn't know where I was, or how I got there, and I couldn't figure out who it was calling me. As I walked down the foggy road, I noticed the voice getting louder, almost as if it were coming directly out of the cavity of my chest, but how could that be?

All of a sudden it got quiet and I couldn't hear it anymore. I remember stopping and looking behind me, but all I could see was fog. When I turned back around, the road had suddenly split. I remember freezing up out of fear, because I didn't know what was going to happen next—things were happening within seconds.

As I walked through the fog, I could faintly see two images. I got closer to the images and was shocked to see that the images looked just like me—they even had pajamas on identical to those I was wearing. "What was going on? Why am I here?" I thought to myself. And why am I staring at images that look just like me? The only difference was one image was smiling and the other image seemed unhappy. My eyes locked upon the sad image's eyes as if a magnet had drawn me to them. I remember staring and wanting to know why he was so unhappy. I was afraid to speak at first, but I finally built up enough courage to ask the images who they were and why they looked just like me. They only stared, but said nothing. Frustrated at their stares I asked again, "Who are you, and why am I here?" Only silence.

I got angry and said, "If this is a joke I don't find it very funny. All I want is to go back home." Still no answer, only the same expressions on their faces. Suddenly I heard the voice again. It said, "Jessie you now have to choose the road in life you want to take. It's left up to you; are you willing to take the journey? It's your choice."

Out of frustration, and being totally confused, I yelled out in despair, "Who are you? Why don't you show your face, you coward? Just show your face!"

The voice replied, "I am the voice of destiny. I am molded and shaped by you, by your thoughts, negative and positive. You make the choice in your life, I only carry them out. Only in you can I be found."

Nervously I said, "I don't understand. Who said that I need you? I didn't ask for you. I was doing just fine before you interrupted my sleep. Just let me go back home, that's all I ask."

The voice only laughed. The sound penetrated throughout my entire body, then it said, "You can't just go home and think that I won't follow you, Jessie. It's not that simple. Whatever you become in life, whatever direction you take, whatever you decide to do, good or bad, I will always be a part of that choice. Whether you want to believe it or not, destiny has knocked at your door. Now it is time to decide your fate."

By that time I was ready to challenge this person calling himself "Destiny." I yelled out, "If you're so tough and such a part of me, come out. Show yourself."

The voice laughed and replied, "How is that possible, Jessie? To show myself is to separate me from you. Only in your actions can I be found. I am a result of what you choose to do in life." Then the voice said again, "Now it is time to decide your fate."

All of a sudden the roads were no longer foggy—they were crystal clear. The two images that looked just like me were both pointing for me to take their road, but I was too confused to decide which one to take. I looked at the image with the smile on his face and thought that maybe I should go down his road. He looked so happy, and according to that thing calling himself destiny, he was a part of me, but the other image was supposed to be a part of me, too, yet he looked so sad. I wondered what was causing him so much pain. I guess my concern for the sadness and pain shown through his eyes got to me, so I finally built up enough courage to choose his road. I looked back toward him and said, "I want to travel down your road." He only stared at me, then he reached out and grabbed my hand; once our hands touched he suddenly disappeared—they both had. Only the split road remained.

Suddenly I heard the voice again. This time it said, "You still have time to change your mind, Jessie, it's left up to you." I looked toward the road I had decided not to choose. I couldn't help but to see that my smiling image had mysteriously reappeared. This time he had a bigger smile on his face, and he no longer had pajamas on. He was wearing one of those expensive silk suits, and was leaning up against a red convertible sports car, my favorite car, and my favorite color. I couldn't take my eyes off of him, but for some strange reason he looked like he had aged. My eyes caught a glimpse of something in his hand. To my amazement I saw that he had the biggest wad of money I think I had ever seen in my life. He kept reaching in his pockets pulling out more. It seemed as if the money had no end. My mind was racing by then. I wondered how he had gotten so much money. I remember thinking to myself that he must have gotten himself a good job, that's it. I began to wonder whether I had picked the right road; after all, the voice said that I could change my mind if I wanted to. I closed my eyes to think, and when I opened them again, to my surprise, the roads were mysteriously posted with signs where they split. At one road, the sign read "the road to riches"; on this road my image of happiness stood. As I looked to my right, posted at this entrance where my image of sadness stood, was "the road to a greater reward." I thought to myself, what could happen next? I was really confused. Then I said to myself, if the reward is so great, then why does this image have such a sad expression on his face? I don't understand how something so great can make someone look so sad, but on the other hand, I've seen part of what the road to riches has to offer. How can I go wrong? That road has to be the road for me—no doubt about it. Through my excitement at my choice, I yelled out, "I've changed my mind. I'm choosing the road to riches."

No answer from the voice. I yelled out again, "Hey, Destiny, I'm on my way, buddy." Still only silence.

I stood still. I noticed that the two images had suddenly reappeared. The image with the sad face was now holding a Bible in his hand. He looked directly in my eyes and at that moment a tear fell from his eye. As the tear hit the ground a white flower miraculously appeared. I was speechless and heard him speak for the first time. He looked directly through the pupils of my eyes and said in a haunting voice, "Jessie, you've now made your decision. Now you must take your journey. Remember what you've seen. Always know that it's never too late to change your heart." He disappeared after he spoke.

His words left me feeling somewhat guilty and feeling sort of empty inside. All of a sudden I was dressed identically to my smiling image—the suit was a perfect fit. It really looked good on me. I immediately bent down and put the white flower that had grown from my other image's teardrop into my lapel. When I raised up from the ground, the split road was now one long road. I couldn't wait to take the journey down my road to riches.

I heard my look-alike say, "Get in the car, Jessie."

I said without hesitation, "Okay, but I want to drive."

He looked at me and said, "You will be driving, Jessie. Don't you know by now that everything I do is what you're really doing or have done? You're only watching yourself. Remember, we're one."

I looked at him and said, "Oh yeah, I keep forgetting. You know, all this is new to me. By the way, what type of work have I found for myself? I must have gone to college or something to be able to afford this car and these expensive clothes, and all of that money I saw in your hand. Let me hold it, smell it or something."

He didn't say anything for a few seconds, then said, "You'll find out soon enough, Jessie." He was looking straight ahead of him at first, then he turned, only staring at me.

I asked him was wrong. He laughed and said, "Nothing is wrong. I just forgot to tell you that you must remember everything you've seen, but it's too late to change your mind."

"What?" I said.

"Why would I want to change my mind? Anyway, my other look-alike said I could, and you're saying I can't. The both of you are confused, if you ask me."

With a sarcastic look on his face, he arrogantly said, "Well, I'm saying you can't, and if you ask me, you're the only confused fool I see. Don't you know by now, Jessie, that I'm the part of you that is deceitful and negative? That pitiful-looking sad-faced image of you was the good part of you. The weak little wimp even had enough nerve to shed a tear over you. For what? The only thing I'll cry over is an onion, but not before taking a bite right out the middle of it." He burst out laughing and said, "You see how weak some people can be? It's funny how what looks a certain way is not how a situation really is."

He kept laughing. His laughter was frightening. I remember screaming for him to let me out of the car, and for him to stop laughing—this was my life, not some make-believe fairytale or joke. He only looked at me with the meanest expression I've ever seen and sped off into the long, dark road. He began to laugh again and was saying over and over, "You were too weak. Now you have to pay the price for it."

I started beating on the car windows, yelling for him to stop the car and let me out. The car doors suddenly locked and I became motionless. I could no longer move; only my image could. Why couldn't I move anymore? Oh my God, I thought, what is happening to me? All I could do now was to sit still and see what my fate was.

I looked ahead of me. I saw that the road was wide and full of curbs. We soon approached a building and the image stopped the car and told me to get out. The street was quiet and empty; there was no one in sight. By now I had finally built up enough nerves to ask him where we were going. He looked at me and arrogantly said, "Stop talking fool; you'll find out soon enough."

Although afraid, I kept saying over and over in my mind that I was not like him, and whatever he does or says will be of his own doing, not mine. I thought about what he said: whatever he does, I have a part in it. Was this really true? If so, then I knew that I had to out-think this negative part of me, and had to do it fast. I thought to myself, what if I started to think positive. What would happen? I feared the image knowing my thoughts as well. Either way, I had to do something. Was my fear of the unknown destiny facing me momentarily giving this negative part of me strength? If so, then I knew that this way of thinking had to change. I really didn't have any other choice, so I decided to release the fear and protect the good in me by destroying the bad. I looked at the image seated next to me and said, "I'm ready to challenge you, because I can't sit still and watch you destroy me the way you'd like to. You may not love yourself, but I choose life. I'm ready to challenge you because I can't stand your attitude, I don't even like being this close to you. All I see is an arrogant, self-centered person who doesn't seem to care about anyone but himself."

He looked at me and said, "You talking to me, boy? I know you couldn't be talking to me. How can you dislike yourself so much, huh, Jessie?"

I quickly replied, "You are not like me. You are the person I never want to become; the person I wouldn't want to face in the mirror each morning; and if it's God's will, I pray that this will be our last meeting."

All of a sudden he started yelling for me to shut up because it was my choice to follow him. He was really upset. Sweat had begun to pop off of his forehead, and his voice began to tremble. He yelled as loud as he could, "You chose the world, Jessie. It was your foolish choice. The decision was yours."

I was speechless as he condemned me, then he said, "And yes, you gambled in your decision to go with me and lost. Now it's too late to turn back."

I could see the strain on his face and the fear in his eyes. I knew the only way to get my life whole within was to face him and not run from the situation. I looked him straight into his eyes as if I were staring at my reflection in the mirror and said, "You won't take me down this road with you, or any other destructive road, because I have faith in knowing that I'm too strong to fall victim to you. I have someone on my side, someone in my heart that I know you can't conquer. With him I can fight this battle with no fear. Because he lives, I can face tomorrow."

All I could hear was laughter, but his eyes were troubled. Through the laughter he said, "You won't win; you've already shown me how weak you are, you little punk. Look at how easily you were drawn to the money and the car. Now you mean to tell me you're ready to challenge me? I don't believe it, and who's this person you're talking about helping you? Don't you know that it's too late to get help? You should have thought about that at first. What do you have to say about that, you weak punk?"

I couldn't wait to answer, and I proudly and courageously said, "It's never too late; you see, I have my heavenly father on my side, and with him I can conquer you, because you can't fight against God. You may find me weak, but with God on my side, strength fills my soul and I have no fear of you."

He suddenly began to scream uncontrollably for me to shut up, but I kept my faith and began to pray out loud to God for help. Throughout his taunting, I prayed repeatedly. The car suddenly started spinning uncontrollably. All of a sudden my image disappeared out of the car; the locks to the doors mysteriously popped up. The empty building we were parked in front of was soon illuminated by lights. Still somewhat dazed, I quickly opened the door of the car and walked up toward the building. I could see a sign on the front, but couldn't make out what it said. My mind was full and I was somewhat confused. I couldn't figure out where my evil image had gone, yet I was glad to be rid of him. All I knew was, when I mentioned God, he vanished before my eyes—just vanished into thin air. I thanked God over and over again for giving me the strength to conquer this negative part of me. As I got closer to the building I was able to read what the sign said. Painted in big black letters was "The Building Of Hope and Everlasting Faith."

The words from the sign filled my soul and my heart was suddenly uplifted. As I approached the door, it slowly opened, and, to my surprise, I saw a figure in the door—my other look-alike, my positive image. In his hand was the Holy Bible, only this time he had a big smile on his face, and his eyes gave so much light that it was difficult to look directly in them. He suddenly extended his hand for me and I extended mine for his. As our hands met, we became one. I felt whole again. I was whole. All of a sudden I could hear spiritual singing coming from inside of the building. The singing rang throughout the night. The Bible pages suddenly flipped out of control by a swift wind that filled the night air, and landed on this verse—Job 5:4: *"For whatsoever is born of God overcometh the world, and this is the victor that overcometh the world, even our faith."*

As I read this verse I was filled with joy and I began to cry, only these were tears of joy. I had fought my father's battle and won. After I gave thanks to the Lord, my curiosity of the building got the better of me. I peeped inside and saw that its structure was incomplete with the exception of a pulpit sitting in the front of the room, filled with a bouquet of white flowers, just like the one that had grown from my image's teardrop. Somehow I knew in the dream that I would see the pulpit again in my life, and when I did, I'd know what my purpose truly was on God's Earth.

I had struggled with my conscience and, with God's help, I had won the battle, but I knew that the battle was not over; yet I have enough faith in God to face tomorrow! In facing tomorrow this question kept weighing heavily on my mind. What was, indeed, my purpose? Or do I truly have one? I'd so often asked myself this, but would soon become frustrated because I wasn't really sure about the answer. I guess it was because I'd always felt that my life had no special significance or meaning, and that I only existed. Strangely enough I'd always hoped that this would change, that I would someday be able to contribute something to mankind, no matter how small. I just wanted to make a difference—a positive difference, that is. There is, indeed, a purpose within my soul's existence. We all have some purpose in life, it's left up to us find out our own courses in life and try to use them positively. We should be proud of who we are, even though, at times, it becomes difficult for us to feel this way. I know this because of what I have experienced. The advice I would give those who feel hopeless is to keep striving. Don't give up, and try not to give in to defeat when life seems to me whipping us from every direction. No one ever said it would be easy, but we sometimes have to make the best of what we've got until we can change our conditions and do better. In doing better we should develop the attitudes of becoming more positive in the total outlook in life. With positive attitudes we will hopefully have a positive effect within our society. Why not encourage those around us to extend a helping hand to those who are in need of help or support? I would not be in the position I'm in today had it not been for those such as Patrick and his family who sort of adopted my family and extended an unselfish welcome for me to be a part of their lives. They were my encouragement.

CHAPTER 10

Sunday, April 8—this blessed day is the beginning of a new path in life. For me, it is my rebirth. Others may say Sunday, April 8, was a day Jessie was reborn.

Mr. Moore was going to be driving us to church so I had to make sure that everyone would be ready on time. All of us had gotten our clothes out the night before, so I knew that would save some time and also keep Willie and Aaron out of each other's face arguing about who's wearing who's underwear. I headed toward Mom's room and knocked on her door. No answer. I knocked again and heard Mom's voice through the crack of the bedroom door, "I'm getting up, son," then she said, "you go on and wake your brothers. I'll get Carmen situated."

I quickly replied, "All right, Mom." I was a nervous wreck. I guessed this wouldn't pass till I was finally at church. Mom's presence at church was going to be very important to me, whether she knew this or not. I had come to really have a lot of respect for her and on this day, my strength was coming through her—she was my hope. Of course we'd had our share of arguments and disagreements, but what mother and son hadn't? Reading Mom's diary had opened my eyes up to a part of what her heart was saying; her innermost desires were put on paper. I found that in some cases I had misjudged her simply because I didn't know what my Mom had gone through, or why she reacted certain ways. Maybe one day I would be able to tell her that I had entered her past by reading her diary. When I do, I want her to know that by entering her past it had cleared up those unanswered questions that had haunted me as a very young boy up until then. I'd even asked myself whether this was God's will for me to discover Mom's diary. I don't know, but I do know that prayer had definitely changed things, and, as a result, I'd seen my family transformed, but not without the help of those special people who are placed in our lives sometimes without us really knowing why. Special people such as Mr. Moore, who had been like a crutch to us; Mama Rose, our second mother; Mr. Charlie, who'd filled our bellies with free food from his store when we didn't have food at home. Patrick's Mom, such an unselfish woman, who loved having a house full of children around; Patrick's dad, Pops, the story-teller and father figure; and not to be left out, my buddy Patrick, who'd has been like a brother. Of course there were many others—my life had not been the same since I had come into contact with these very special people.

My thoughts were soon interrupted by snoring coming from the bedroom where Willie and Aaron were sleeping; waking those two knuckleheads was going to be my morning workout. I quickly put my plan into motion. I entered the bathroom and wet two towels with cold water; this always worked for Mom on me. I dreaded the moment she'd slap those cold towels across my face—most of the time in the middle of a good dream. Once I got so angry when she did it that I threw the towel without looking and hit Mom in the face. I still feel the stings from the belt: my butt stayed sore for about a week. Now it was my turn to battle with those brothers of mine.

After getting Willie and Aaron up with the help of the wet towels and a threat or two, I hurried into the kitchen to fix their cereal. I didn't have time to listen to them argue over who was going to get the prize out of the cereal box this time. Their mornings were not normal unless they were at each other's throat about something. I grabbed a clean glass out of the sink and poured myself some milk.

After gulping it down I rushed Willie and Aaron through breakfast. I knew Mom and Carmen would be ready soon. I had already taken Mom's toast and coffee to her and fixed Carmen's cereal. I just had to keep an eye on those brothers of mine. That little knucklehead, Willie, had already gotten angry with me because I had told him to stop talking and finish eating. I got one of his "I can't stand you" looks and a smart remark to top it off. With cereal falling out of his mouth and his chin almost in the bowl, he looked upside my head and said, "Why are you always telling us what to do, always bossing us around like you're our dad or something? I'll be glad when I'm grown; you won't tell me what to do then, because I'll put a knot upside your head."

Aaron started laughing and joined in by saying, "Yeah, Jessie, when we get big enough, me and Willie gonna kick your butt for always bossing us around. Nobody's gonna tell us what to do because we'll kick their butts, too! We'll be able to eat anything we want to eat."

Willie interrupted Aaron. Talking with his mouth full of cereal, he said, "That's right, and we won't have nobody telling us when to clean up. We gonna do what we want to and if you come over to our house trying to boss us around we'll just pop you in the nose and slam the door in your face like Mom did when that man came who said he was the landlord yelling about the rent money. She slammed the door right against his nose."

Aaron picked up his bowl and started to drink the leftover milk from it, but not without making loud, slurping sounds. I told him to stop eating like a pig; he only slurped louder, the little smart-mouth. He looked sideways at me and said, "Yeah, Jessie, me and Willie gonna have us a big house on a hill with a big mean-looking dog named Sampson. We gonna make him chase off people we don't want at our house, and we ain't getting married, 'cause we don't need no wife telling us what to do; we just gonna have a bunch of girlfriends."

Willie started laughing and said, "And if any of our girlfriends make us mad we'll just sic our dog on them, too!"

Aaron laughed and said, "Yeah, Willie, we don't need no ashy-legs girlfriends, anyway. They talk too much." Then he said, "We gonna be rich, too, Jessie. Gonna have our own business."

I looked at him and said, "Oh really? What kind of business would you two bullies run talking about kicking everybody's butt? You'd better not let me hear either one of you say that again. I see now that I've got to get you two in line before one of you gets into some serious trouble."

They both looked at each other, then Aaron leaned over and whispered, thinking that I couldn't hear, and told Willie that I was acting like a bootleg father.

I ignored what I'd heard and asked them again what kind of business they planned on opening. Willie looked at me with his chest stuck out and said, "We gonna sell Kool-Aid, pickles and hotdogs to people when they get hungry. We gonna be unclemanures like Mr. Charlie. When we make enough money we gonna open up a bunch of stores with all kinds of stuff in it."

I couldn't hold the laughter in any longer. Those two were something else—big words and all. I told them that Mr. Charlie was an "entrepreneur" and that they had given him a new name.

Not to be outdone, Willie yelled out, "That's what I said, you old tank-head church boy. I hope your head doesn't keep you from being baptized today. It's too big to go under water without floating."

They both burst out laughing. I grabbed the cereal bowls off the table and told them to get dressed for church, and that if they didn't stop running their smart little mouths that I was going to put both of them in double headlocks and drag them in church with what they had on—their underwear and t-shirts. The headlock threat worked every time. Patrick and I got a kick out of wrestling with them. We'd throw them around like Frisbees through the air. This was exciting to them. It gave them a chance to also show off their homemade karate skills. What they hated most was for us to put them in headlocks—those little jokers would be bent over, squirming and kicking their legs all over the place, then one of them would get angry and start biting at the air. It was hilarious.

My next move was to do what they really hated. I'd take my balled-up fist and briskly rub it across their heads and run with heads fastened within the grip of my arm as if charging into a tree or brick wall. I'd release them within inches of whatever we were in front of. Once they caught their breath from being scared stupid they would chase me and Patrick, sometimes crying because they were so angry. Once they threw bricks at us, missing my head by an inch. The last time me and Patrick headlocked them, Willie and Aaron got their revenge by tying my feet up with a rope while I was asleep and also one of my arms to the bedpost. When I woke up, they let me have it. Willie yelled out, "We got you now, you big sissy. Patrick's next." Before I knew it I felt something striking me across the head. Aaron had made nunchucks out of smoke sausages and was beating me upside my head with them. With my free arm, I was able to grab a hold of them, but not before Willie jumped across the bed with a pillow in his hand and started whacking me across the head again. They both went for my head, trying to put me a headlock. I was laughing and yelling for them to stop, at the same time still swinging at them with one arm. I finally get a good grip on Willie's legs. He started to yell, "I give up, Jessie. I give up, Jessie."

Without warning, he backed his butt in my face and let out this loud fart, which smelled horribly. I was in a life-or-death situation with his enemy gas; I had to show him who was in charge. I got him around the waist and held on to him as tightly as I could even though I was still sort of dazed from them popping me upside my head with those pillows. Willie started yelling for Aaron to help him. Aaron charged for the bed. By that time Mom was in the room with her belt. She was upset because her sleep had been interrupted and she was also yelling, "What the Hell is going on in here?"

Her focus was then on Aaron, who was standing next to my bed with her lunch in his hands—his nunchuck-smoked sausages, her favorite hotdogs. I was tied to the bed and Willie, as usual, was going to try to lie his and Aaron's way out of this one. They looked at Mom, who angrily yelled, "I said, what is going on in here? I'm trying to rest on my day off and wake up to what sounds like a war zone." She angrily looked at me, gritted her teeth, and said, "Jessie, I said, what is going on in here?"

I blurted out, "Ask those two maniacs. All I know is I woke up tied to the bed and they were smacking me with smoked sausages and pillows."

Mom's attention soon focused back on Aaron. She yelled, "Aaron, what are you doing with those smoked-sausages in your hands? Now I know you've lost your mind as hard as it is making ends meet you've got the nerve to take meat and play with it."

Aaron started to stutter, a familiar habit when he was nervous or afraid, too scared to say anything, he just stood looking pitifully at Mom.

Willie built up enough courage to point at me and say, "Jessie put us in a headlock the other day, so we were paying him back."

Mom told them to untie me. I was trying to get Mom's sympathy, so I put on this innocent look to keep her off of my case. After being untied, Mom seemed to inspect the room. She put her hand on her hip as she often did when making a point, and said, "Both of you, out. I see you all didn't learn your lesson the last time I spanked you for throwing dishes at each other. Willie, go get my belt, and you, Aaron, get your little butt in the hall."

They both got sore butts that morning. I got lectured on wrestling too roughly with them and encouraging them by laughing while they were clowning around. No punishment was handed down to me that morning. I guess Mom figured I had already gotten my punishment—the wrath of Willie and Aaron. I knew then, as I know today, that when all the fun is over and when any of us step out into the dangers and temptations of the real world, that I've got to keep a close eye, not only on my brothers, but Mom and Carmen, as well.

I was also trying to encourage them to never give up on things when it seemed difficult for them. I continued to help them with their homework and oftentimes would ask them what they planned to do when they graduated from school and college. I preferred to use the word "when" with them instead of "if."

I tried to reflect, as much as I could, positive images for them. They might have a long road ahead of them, but my brothers and sister would hopefully be able to boast about a brother who had helped them as much as possible to carry the load that comes with the everyday struggles of life. Joseph was called the dreamer. I told them that when they allow others to stifle their dreams or blow out their candle of hope, then they allow their own desires to flicker out. I also told them that without a goal in life or some foundation to build on, they might soon perish in that they allowed their lives to be non-existent and to always keep their flames of life burning brightly.

Another positive boost is for them to share this positive light with others. Last, but not least, I explained to them that there is no mountain too high to climb, or any goal too hard to reach with a little hope and desire. These two ingredients, they understand, will be their substance of growth and that they should always have a desire to plant seeds of hope in the minds of others and to always stay focused in their innermost desires. As Mr. Moore says, plant seeds of positive growth and in planting those seeds man will indeed see changes take place. Those seeds can be their voices crying out for positive changes, and can definitely make a difference.

So many thoughts were running through my mind, it dawned on me at that point that I had to get Willie and Aaron ready. After inspecting their clothes, I headed for the bathroom, almost bumping into Mom and Carmen as they were making their exit. Mom looked at me, smiled, and said, "Well, Jessie, your day has finally come. I never did think I'd ever step foot in any church, but God's divine intervention has miraculously made itself known through you!"

With tears in her eyes she leaned over, hugged me and said, "I'm so proud of you; all of us are. There's so much good in you. You have been the strength of this family and you've held us together. I know it's been difficult and you've shed many tears when you thought I wasn't looking, but through the pain you kept fighting and struggling to keep this family together, always being here for us."

She grabbed the bottom of my chin as she always does when she wants to get a point across or be heard, looking directly in my eyes, and said, "Just wanted you to know that we love you, son!"

Carmen grabbed one of my legs and hugged it tightly, gently laying her head on my thigh, and said, "I love Jessie, too, Mommy."

I felt myself becoming emotional, but before I could say anything, Mom reached for Carmen, who still had her little arms fastened around my thighs, and said, "Come on, baby, let your brother get ready. We don't want to make him late for church." Mom smiled once more at me, leaving me standing in the bathroom door.

For a split-second I stood in a daze, but snapped back to reality after remembering that Mr. Moore would be here to pick us up. I immediately closed the door, got out of my pajamas and took a quick shower. After brushing my teeth I grabbed for the comb and brush. I wanted to make sure I looked my best for church. I found myself at one point staring at my reflection in the mirror, not out of vainness, but of having a part of me reflecting itself in a different light. I felt special—so much had happened within the last few months and I had actually gotten to know myself: the person, not the shell, who had been, at one point, empty of all hope and desires in life. I was now the Jessie who no longer thought of himself as an unwanted young black male, but through God's grace my eyes had been opened. Life no longer appeared to me as meaningless. Instead, life now had become a mission. Whereas the days ahead of me, at one point, had appeared cloudy and gray, now God's ray of sunshine abounded me by filling my heart with a rainbow no man could ever duplicate. Within this rainbow, I'd found the true colors of life, ever-changing within my kaleidoscope of hope.

Mom was so right when she spoke about God's intervention. My life had evolved when I had found Him. He'd been with me when I didn't even know it. With so many thoughts flowing through my mind I could have easily lost track of time, but not today. I rushed out of the bathroom, catching a quick glimpse of Willie and Aaron putting their socks and shoes on. I could hear Mom telling Carmen to sit still and not get dirty. Then I heard the familiar "Willie, Aaron, are you two dressed?" And, as if on cue, they yelled, "Yes, mama."

Mom was asking them about their hair. "Did y'all comb and brush your hair?" Before they could answer, Mom was saying, "Come in here and let me take a look at you two."

Willie moaned, "Aw, man," and they headed toward the living room. Surprisingly enough I heard Mom telling them how nice they looked. She said they looked like two little businessmen with their neckties on. Mama Rose had given us neckties last Christmas and this was the first time Willie and Aaron had worn theirs. I'd worn mine the first time I'd visited Patrick's church. I remembered feeling sort of awkward when I first walked inside the church. I felt like I wasn't worthy enough to be there—my own feelings of insecurity, I guess.

Within minutes of being greeted and introduced to so many people, those feelings had quickly faded away. My eyes glimpsed the Bible Patrick had given me, lying on the dresser. I reached for it, gazing upon the engraved letters, "Jessie Fremont." Little did I know when I received this precious book how it would be a tool of purpose for me.

Before leaving the room to join the rest of the family, I had to take one deep breath and say a quick prayer. My stomach was rumbling with nervousness, but I knew that this would be short-lived.

I heard a horn blowing outside. I knew it was Mr. Moore. Mom could be heard yelling, "Jessie, our ride is here." Willie and Aaron bolted out of the door like lightning; Mom and Carmen were next. After locking the door, I found myself racing down the steps for the car. Everyone was smiling and gazing upon me as if I were a celebrity or something. I felt so special that morning.

I grabbed for the car door's handle. Carmen was squealing about sitting in my lap. I grabbed her, placed her in my lap and buckled the seatbelt. My next chore was to move her long braids out of my face; because, if I didn't, those braids armed with barrettes were like tiny weapons, attacking my face whenever Carmen turned her little head.

I reached over and shook Mr. Moore's hand, thanking him for picking us up. He, of course, said, "You know I don't mind, son. I wouldn't miss your baptism for anything in the world. You've made me very proud of you. A man couldn't ask for a better son than one like you." He reached up for the rearview mirror, looking through it to get a glimpse of Mom, then said, "Isn't that right, Betty?"

I turned to look at Mom, and she was actually blushing. There was definitely something brewing up between those two. It was those funny looks they gave each other. Mom looked at me and said, "That's right. Jessie has made all of us so proud of him. I just told him this back at the house. I do have to admit that, through the troubled waters, Jessie has been the one who has held this family together and steered us in the right direction." Still speaking with tears in her eyes, Mom said, "God has truly been working with us through Jessie, and to think that I, of all people, his mother, fought so hard against my son attending church. So many mothers and fathers are encouraging their children to attend church, even pick up a Bible, for the simple fact that they don't. I have so much to be forgiven for," she said.

I responded by telling Mom that I understood and didn't hold any grudges. I reassured her that the she had made me proud of her in many ways and not to blame herself for anything. More importantly, that all of us would be at church today.

Mr. Moore said, "That's right, Betty. Stop blaming yourself or beating yourself across the back. All of us have made mistakes, or said and done something wrong, but in the process we correct those wrongs and learn from them and forge ahead."

As he spoke he reached for the knob on the car radio, but not before asking Mom whether it was all right to listen to some gospel music. Mom blushed and said, "Of course not, Mitchell. Anyway, we're the passengers in your car. You have the right to listen to whatever you normally do when we're not in here with you."

Mr. Moore smiled and said, "Well, I thought I'd be a gentlemen and ask anyway. This may be my car, but there's still room for common courtesy. I was once told that we should never take anyone for granted or assume that it's okay to do certain things or act certain ways because we feel we're in the driver's seat, so to speak." Mr. Moore always had a way with making the other person feel comfortable even the shyest of people; I've seen him do it so many times at school. He was just a natural at motivating people.

My thoughts soon went from Mr. Moore to the song playing on the radio. It really caught my attention—the lyrics were so meaningful—and it was as if the song had been dedicated to me. I asked Mr. Moore what the name of the song was. He looked at me and said, "Son, this song is called "God's Rainbow." It happens to be one of my favorites. As a matter of fact, I've sort of based my work and life on those lyrics, in helping the children and families as much as I can."

I nodded my head as he spoke and listened more intently to the song which had so much meaning, in particular, when the singer sang about helping mankind find peace in the wake of life's storm. The song was beautiful. I made a point to remember the name of it, because I knew I would end of buying it at the record store.

The ride to the church was one of anticipation. As we pulled onto the church's parking lot, I felt myself become sort of lightheaded. I also had to deal with the loud rumbling within the pit of my stomach. The palms of my hands became sweaty, and I found myself loosening my necktie. Mr. Moore must have sensed my nervousness because he asked me whether I was all right. Trying to stay composed, I replied, "I'm fine—just a little hot."

Mr. Moore looked at me and jokingly said, "More like nervous, wouldn't you say?" Then he said, "Just take a deep breath and relax."

Mom reached over the car seat and gently rubbed the top of my shoulders and said, "Jessie, you're here now, son." Straightening my necktie,

Mom kept talking, looking me directly in my eyes. She smiled and said, "This is your day, so don't get nervous and faint on us now. Anyway, you're too tall for me to be thinking about trying to lift up off the ground." Seeing Mom in such a relaxed state sort of eased my own tension. I took her advice and quickly made my way out of the car.

Upon entering the church, I caught a glimpse of Patrick and his Dad, Pop. Patrick's Mom was seated next to Pop and was pointing in the direction of the pew in the front of them. As I made my way down the aisle, Mama Rose was the first to grab me. She made a point to let me know that she would not have missed my baptism for anything in the world. I thanked her for coming and headed toward the bathroom—nervousness always sent me to the toilet. With us arriving early it gave me the opportunity to mingle. I shook so many hands that morning that my wrist began to ache. There was so much love flowing through church that morning. It felt good knowing that I had also found new friends.

Soon afterwards, everyone was seated. As the preacher approached the podium, a silent hush filled the church. Once he began to speak, his voice seemed to penetrate the air. He spoke with such eloquence and he preached such a thought-provoking sermon.

As his voice roared throughout the church, he asked the congregation this question, "Are you your brother's keeper?" I didn't understand what he meant at first, but as he kept preaching his words became clear to me. Strangely enough it seemed as if he was preaching about my life. I felt his sermon that morning should have caused quite a few people to question their own purpose while here on Earth. Indeed, for me, the sermon was timely. Had it not been for those who considered themselves to be their brother's keeper, I would not be sitting in church today. God only knows what would have happened to me without the help of these wonderful people who unselfishly reached out over and over to lend a helping hand in times of need to me and my family.

Soon the invitation for those wanting to be baptized was extended. Those wanting to be baptized made their way to the front of the church. As I rose from the pew my eyes met Mom's. I immediately bent down and kissed her, ever so gently, on her cheek. With tears welling up in her eyes, Mom whispered, "I love you, son,"

Mr. Moore reached over and shook my hand. I noticed Mama Rose wiping tears from her eyes. Carmen could be heard asking, "Where's Jessie going?"

Once I made my way to the front of the church, I noticed two large planters filled with the most beautiful white flowers. For a moment I froze in my steps. There was a familiar sense of being in this room somehow in spiritual way. I found myself drawn to the flowers and suddenly realized that those flowers were identical to the flowers that had appeared in the dream I'd had. At that moment I started to feel my insides tremble, and my jaws started to shake such as they did when I was in cold weather. I felt sort of like I was moving in slow motion.

After finally making my way to the front church pew, I sat motionless and watched the two people before me being baptized. I couldn't help but study the expressions on their faces, which seemed to change from that of almost a blank expression to one of joy after they had emerged from the baptismal waters and been pulled out.

I was next; it felt like the eyes of the entire congregation were on me, sort of like their eyes were piercing my soul. I only stared upon the waters in the baptismal pool. My knees started to tremble and I started to feel sort of lightheaded, but nothing was going to stop me now. Time seemed suspended as my feet guided themselves toward the baptismal pool, and before I knew it I was standing within the same water that I'd watched the others be submerged in. The hand of the deacon raised itself toward Heaven, and again the deacon said, "I baptize you in the name of the Father, the Son, and the Holy Ghost." As I fell back within the water, I felt my body go limp and my life seemed to rush before me. The waters gushed throughout my ears. I felt at peace. I can't explain why it felt so safe while in the water, but within seconds I was snatched from the waters by the large hands of the deacon—snatched out of the water such as a baby being pulled from its mother's womb. Only this time, instead of being born into a world of sin, I was instead being cleansed of sin. My rebirth as a new child in Christ had finally taken place. At that moment, I felt invincible, I can't begin to explain my sense of empowerment, but I was on a spiritual high. I felt at peace. So much peace that I wondered how long it would last.

    I knew that in the days to come I would be tested and challenged in many ways, but there was peace in knowing that I had a Father in Heaven who would continue to watch over me. The test of my faith was within my own conscious being of defining right from wrong, and good versus evil. God didn't have to test me; he already knew my strengths and weakness. The creator of all knows all. Whoever said life would come without trials? Indeed, if life were that simple, we, in turn, would feel no need to fall upon our knees or cry out to our Father in Heaven. Mankind would eventually become extinct due to the moral fiber of society becoming stained by the sin of the self-destructive man. Whatever awaited me outside of those church doors, only God knew, but it would be left up to me to make the right choices at the crossroads in my life.

This was a new chapter in my life, and I prayed for peace within my family.

After church my mother and Carmen were the first to greet me. They both ran over with arms extended. We all embraced and, at that moment, no words were spoken—only hugs, smiles and kisses. Mom was the first to speak. Excitedly she said, "Jessie, you've opened my heart to what I've always known, that God is love and works miracles." I know now that neither me, nor anyone else, could interfere with God's plan for you." Then she spoke these words that I'll never forget, "Jessie, whether you know this or not, you've already opened my heart to what I've always known, but chose to turn away from because of something that happened in my life years ago. I chose to turn my back on religion, but I know that God has worked through you to bring me back home. He's used you, son, to open my heart."

Mom kept talking and I listened. She didn't realize that I already understood what she was trying to say. Mom cleared her throat and seemed somewhat hesitant to keep talking, almost as if she couldn't find the right words, then she said, "Jessie, there is something I need to talk with you about. Hopefully you'll understand why I've kept some things away from you that you had a right to know about."

Grabbing both of my hands and rubbing the top of my knuckles Mom nervously said, "Jessie, you've already shown me that there is light at the end of the tunnel of life's uncertain paths. Now it is time for me to shine some of the light you've given me back into your direction. Hopefully you'll find your way through this maze of confusion I've created."

As Mom spoke these words she began to cry. I leaned over and hugged her and told her that whatever she needed to talk with me about could wait. Willie and Aaron were headed our way. Patrick was pulling the car around to the front of the church to keep Mama Rose from having to walk across the large parking lot—he knew her legs gave out on her easily. Within minutes, the most important people surrounded me in my life—my family and friends, Willie and Aaron, extending their hands for me to shake.

All of a sudden, Mom blurted out, "Your brothers told me about those handshakes in the best way they could." She asked me to tell her what was going on. Willie yelled out, "It's our secret, Mom. This is man stuff."

Carmen started to laugh and said, "Jessie, Willie's not a man; he's a midget." Aaron couldn't let his brother down; he struck back at Carmen with, "Who's she calling a midget? She's so short she wears a sock for a turtleneck." Mama Rose was nearby and started to pull cookies out of her purse. We knew she was going to stuff them with cookies. This was a habit of hers: to silence them by feeding them silly.

Mom and I kept talking. We knew that, through all the fussing, those three were not happy unless they were at each other's throats. I told Mom that those handshakes were our bond and that I had told Willie and Aaron that this bond was one which would take us beyond an earthly nature of brotherhood to one of a Christian brotherhood. Those handshakes were their promise to me that they would someday be baptized once they came to the point of knowing the true meaning of baptism.

Mom's face lit up with joy. She looked at me and said, "There's one more hand you have to shake, son."

Puzzled at her statement, I asked, "Whose hand did I not shake?"

Mom winked and extended her hand to mine, then said, "Although the hugs were nice, it's time for me to bond with you on a Christian journey. You got enough room for one more person?" We both started laughing, still holding hands, which evolved in a son and mother hugging one another as time stood still for them to bathe in the glory of God's divine intervention.

As I left church that morning with my brothers clinging to my side and my buddy Patrick slapping me across the back, I knew that my battle was just beginning. Patrick and I marched on that day, both of us hard-fighting soldiers on the battlefield. The battlefield is the war of good versus evil. Ignorance and lack of enlightenment is now ever-present in the schools, in our neighborhoods, our parks, even within the sanctity of our homes. Our weapon in fighting these battles is one of evolving within the chaotic maze of ignorance and self-hatred. Man, which is mind, must direct one's footsteps toward stepping into an illuminated path. Where there is enlightenment, ignorance will soon diminish itself into oblivion. And as man peers within the reflective mirror(s) of life; consider the reflection peering back as the eye gazes upon itself. Generations of preconceived thoughts and misconceptions peer and linger within the minds' window. Darkness glooms, yet enlightenment prevails. Consider the source within the attic of your mind as you evolve and transcend within a dimension above all others. Time beckons itself to a journey in which enlightenment greets the traveler seeking wisdom, as understanding sheds light on the source of true existence. As I've journeyed this difficult road with family and friends, I give honor to my higher power. I now consider myself to be an intricate part of this omnipotent being, as I've also discovered my own source of strength.

My source of enlightenment, which is my dwelling place of inner peace, I honor in my higher power's name. Within this manifestation of a new age, which has come. I purpose my own existence, as thy will be done. While on this planet, as it is within, this dimension of bliss, I choose to transcend. In bestowing time, I greet this day with the sustenance of wisdom along the way. And while conquering my own weaknesses, I am able to pardon the weaknesses of others. Yet I choose not to be led within a microcosmic Christian struggle. Having been set free from the abyss of darkness, I revel within the cosmic sphere of a kingdom which rules the heart of man, while deliverance of ignorance abounds itself to a more enlightened land. Desiring not to be led astray with the enticement of ignorance, allows one to be set free from the snares of darkness, and so it shall be. Within this

LeNora Millen

time and space, man welcomes the appointed hour, for within my world, my kingdom is one of illumination and magnificent power.

It is, and so it shall be. . . . forever!

The beginning . . .

ABOUT THE AUTHOR

LeNora, a native Memphian is a graduate of Northside High School and holds a Masters degree in Business and plans to pursue her Doctorate. An avid reader herself, LeNora feels that through writing, she is able to express more of her creative self. Although Seeds of Deception is a fiction, the axiom, art imitating life and life imitating art comes into play either directly or indirectly. The book was written from the perspective of a fourteen year old and LeNora hopes to convey a message of courage, strength and hope.

Printed in the United States
29484LVS00003B/58-111